SHERLOCK HOLMES
and the HOLMES
BAKER STREET IRREGULARS

SHERLOCK HOLMES

and the

BAKER STREET IRREGULARS

B · S · I

The Fall of the Amazing Zalindas

CASEBOOK Nº 1

By Tracy Mack and Michael Citrin

Illustrations by Greg Ruth

ORCHARD BOOKS · NEW YORK
An Imprint of Scholastic Inc.

Among the many sources we consulted while researching this book,
the following were especially important in helping us understand Sherlock Holmes and his world,
Victorian London, and circus life in nineteenth-century England:
The Annotated Sherlock Holmes by Sir Arthur Conan Doyle, edited by
William S. Baring-Gould; *The New Annotated Sherlock Holmes* by Sir Arthur Conan Doyle,
edited by Leslie S. Klinger; *Sherlock Holmes: The Man and His World* by H. R. F. Keating;
The Sherlock Holmes Scrapbook, edited by Peter Haining; *What Jane Austen Ate and
Charles Dickens Knew* by Daniel Pool; *The Writer's Guide to Everyday Life in Regency and Victorian
England from 1811–1901* by Kristine Hughes; *Victorian People and Ideas* by Richard D. Altick;
London Characters and Crooks by Henry Mayhew; *Victorian Studio Photographs* by Bevis Hillier;
and *Seventy Years a Showman* by "Lord" George Sanger.

Text copyright © 2006 by Tracy Mack and Michael Citrin
Illustrations copyright © 2006 by Greg Ruth
All rights reserved. Published by Orchard Books, an imprint of Scholastic Inc.
ORCHARD BOOKS and design are registered trademarks of Watts Publishing Group, Ltd.,
used under license. SCHOLASTIC and associated logos are trademarks and/or registered
trademarks of Scholastic Inc.

Library of Congress Cataloging-in-Publication Data
Mack, Tracy. Citrin, Michael.
The fall of the Amazing Zalindas / Tracy Mack and Michael Citrin.
p. cm. – (Sherlock Holmes and the Baker Street Irregulars; casebook no. 1)
Summary: The ragamuffin boys known as the Baker Street Irregulars help Sherlock Holmes solve
the mysterious deaths of a family of circus tightrope walkers.
ISBN 0-439-82836-8 (hardcover)
[1. Circus – Fiction. 2. Great Britain – History – 19th century – Fiction. 3. Mystery and detective
stories.] I. Citrin, Michael. Mack, Tracy. II. Title. III. Series: Sherlock Holmes
and the Baker Street Irregulars ; casebook no. 1.
PZ7.M18995Fa 2006 [Fic] – dc22 2005034000

10 9 8 7 6 5 4 3 2 1   06 07 08 09 10
Printed in the U.S.A. 23
Reinforced Binding for Library Use • First edition, September 2006
Book design by Elizabeth B. Parisi

To Martin Citrin,

for his introduction to

the Master and his methods,

and to Ruby Citrin,

for filling every day

with mystery and grand adventure

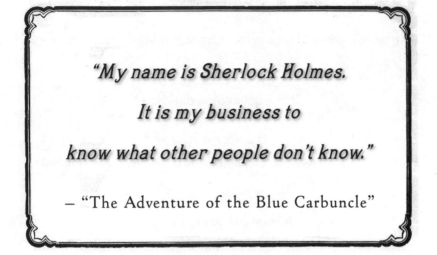

"My name is Sherlock Holmes.

It is my business to

know what other people don't know."

— "The Adventure of the Blue Carbuncle"

Contents

Esteemed Reader,

I am told that children (and many grown-ups), even intelligent ones, do not read prefaces, finding them too dull or pointless. But I assure you, I am not one to tarry over frivolities, and I ask you to indulge me in providing a few details regarding the world you are about to enter.

PREFACE
In which you will discover
some fascinating information

First, we shall be traveling to the final years of Victorian England, a time of tradition and change, of industry and ideas — the last chapter of an empire. Before you dismiss this as a boring history lesson, before you roll your eyes and shut the book on me, read a bit further. For I shall share with you never-before-documented adventures involving one of the greatest minds of the day.

If you have not by now heard of the world's finest consulting detective, Mr. Sherlock Holmes, you have undoubtedly spent your years beneath a large rock, or perhaps you've been raised by wolves in the wild. I speak of the most brilliant and celebrated crime solver of all time — the model for modern crime detection!

Much has been written about Mr. Holmes. In fact, in total there are fifty-six short stories and four novels that tell of his adventures in great detail. They were recorded by Holmes's friend and biographer, Dr. John Watson. While entertaining, Watson's stories are *not* entirely accurate. It would be mean-spirited of me to blame the inconsistencies and curious oversights on Watson, who was well intentioned and probably thought he was providing a faithful account of Holmes's adventures. But one particular omission has produced a grave injustice.

Everyone familiar with Mr. Holmes knows that he did not work alone. An extremely enthusiastic and loyal gang of homeless boys were part of his organization. They were called the Baker Street Irregulars, and they assisted Mr. Holmes in countless cases and provided spectacular services in his crime solving. And yet, the Irregulars are mentioned in less than a handful of Watson's stories.

We will never know whether Watson intended to glorify Holmes alone (and by extension himself). But no matter one's opinion on the reasons for this shortcoming, it is a shameful omission indeed. All history needs some correction, and now it's time the Baker Street Irregulars have their due.

Are you not curious about this gang of street sleuths? The leaders: Ozzie, with his brilliant mind, and Wiggins, whose street smarts outfoxed the toughest criminals. Rohan the gentle giant, Elliot the ruffian, the tiny lad Alfie, and others. Would you not like to know them? Do you not agree it is time that you and the rest of the world learn the truth?

Surely it is.

You may be wondering who I am to make such assertions and to take on such a responsibility. Let us just say that I stand as a witness, and the truth of what I tell shall ring loudly to all those who are willing to hear it.

But I won't waste any more of your time. Let me share the story, and you can decide for yourself.

Before you turn the page, I must warn you that you are about to enter a world of death and danger, greed and deception, and an evil more potent than lightning. This story is not for the faint of heart, nor those of feeble spirit. But I hope you will be brave enough not to turn back now.

Read on, pay close attention, and you may yet discover who I am. As Sherlock Holmes said, "The world is full of obvious things which nobody by any chance observes."

Yours anonymously

London, England

CHAPTER ONE
Three gruesome deaths

L adies and gentlemen, lads and lasses, I take you now to the dangerous heights of the tightrope — the boldest show act of all time! — some twelve spans above us. . . ."

Avalon Barboza, the ringmaster of the Grand Barboza Circus, stood proudly in the center of the Big Top. He and his show folk had been traveling throughout England for the past seven months and were now performing in St. John's Wood in London. The year was 1889, the month September, and a light rain pricked the tent top, causing the naphtha lamps to dim and swell on that chilly autumn evening.

Dressed in a black velvet tunic trimmed with gold bugles, white turndown collar and linen cuffs, cream-colored knee breeches, and black Hessian boots, Barboza pointed his bronze staff at the tightrope strung near the very top of the tent. His black velvet hat carried three ostrich feathers, and beneath it his long blond hair and mustache had been perfectly curled with curling tongs. He pattered to his audience in an accent of Eastern European flavor.

"... The zenith of our tent, as tall as a great ship's mast, reaches an altitude at which no man was meant to travel. Picture yourselves at such a dizzying height and asked to walk a mere rope!"

As Barboza gestured, two men climbed quick as spiders up the center support Pole, which stood between two rings that circled the floor of the tent. At the outer edge of one of the rings, a third man climbed with similar agility up another pole. Once they reached the tops of the poles, the men balanced on narrow perches. They wore white sequined fleshings that hugged their muscular frames, and from the stands far below, they looked like snow monkeys.

"Human beings were not designed to travel at such heights. But these rare specimens are made more of air than earth," Barboza continued. "Such men fear no gravity; in fact, their minds are free from apprehension of any kind. You are about to witness the unparalleled daring of such men. Ladies and gentlemen, lads and lasses, I give you none other than the world-renowned, the Amazing Zalindas!"

Applause rang through the tent as Wolfgang Zalinda stepped onto the rope, holding a long pole. He took steady strides and walked with ease to the middle of the rope. Then, pointing his toe like a dancer, he slid his right foot forward and kissed the rope with his left knee before standing again. The audience gasped and then applauded.

From a break in the stands, a darkened figure watched with particular interest. He paced and stroked his bald head, grinding his teeth angrily. Barboza's words were like a dagger in his heart. "Arrogance is its own curse," he whispered to himself, and then spit bile from his mouth.

Meanwhile, Wilhelm and Werner Zalinda stepped onto the rope at the same time from opposite directions. Werner carried a chair, which he obtained from a rack above the perch.

"Not one ropewalker, ladies and gentlemen, not two, not three, but four . . . er, rather, not two, but three!" yelled Barboza.

Wilhelm and Werner reached the midpoint of the rope at the same time. Wilhelm scrambled up the front of Wolfgang and drew himself into a squatting position on his shoulders.

From a break in the stands, a darkened figure watched with particular interest.

Then he turned himself around 180 degrees and stood. The brothers were now facing the same direction, making a human tower. The crowd buzzed and clapped loudly.

From behind them, Werner Zalinda handed the chair around to Wilhelm, who placed the back legs on his shoulders and clasped the front legs in his fists. Werner climbed up the backs of Wolfgang and Wilhelm until he was standing on Wilhelm's shoulders, his feet placed purposefully between the chair legs. He held his arms aloft, then placed his palms on the back of the chair, leapt over it, and landed in a sitting position on the seat. He opened his arms wide like wings and raised his legs in a graceful pike position.

The crowd went wild. It was only half past eight, and already the Zalindas were the stars of the evening.

From behind a curtain, another darkened figure watched and cursed the brothers. He drew a small bottle from his coat pocket, tipped his head, swigged, and swallowed. He stifled a mirthless laugh and, as he watched the tightrope, he muttered to himself, "Death to all of you."

The wind kicked up outside, causing the lamps to flicker. In that moment, as if the figure's words had suddenly come alive, the Zalindas' steadiness seemed to falter. Though the movement was slight, the rope appeared to be sinking.

Werner Zalinda leapt from the chair back onto Wilhelm's shoulders, causing the chair to tumble backward. It looked for all the world like a spinning toy, until it cracked into pieces on the tent floor.

A nervous chatter rumbled in the stands, and then a loud tearing sound ripped through the tent.

The Zalindas had no time to dismantle their tower before the unraveling tightrope snapped beneath their feet. The single unit of their bodies tilted forward, then separated as the brothers fell swiftly and soundlessly. So practiced was their timing, so instinctual were their movements that their limbs flapped and shuddered in harmony with one another, like three ducks shot in mid-flight. Their bodies hit the floor in perfect synchronicity. Blood soaked the sawdust, forming the distinct impression of a slightly crooked letter *M*.

A few rows up in the stands, a well-dressed stranger casually left his seat and, with a swing of his cane, exited the tent.

CHAPTER TWO
An important visitor seeks assistance from Sherlock Holmes

In the heart of London's posh West End, just south of the circus grounds, approximately twelve hours later, a husky, round-faced boy called Wiggins stood proudly on Baker Street, singing in a high falsetto:

> *"Here's a health to the queen and a lasting peace,*
> *To fraction an end, to wealth increase;*
> *Come let us drink it while we have breath,*
> *For there's no drinking after death,*
> *And he that will this health deny,*
>
> *"Down among the dead men,*
> *Down among the dead men,*
> *Down, down, down, down,*
> *Down among the dead men,*
> *Let him lie. . . ."*

The city folk seemed to appreciate Ozzie's asthma more than Wiggins's singing.

Wiggins's friend, Osgood Manning, sat beside him with an old bowler hat turned upward, hugging his bony knees and looking pitifully into the eyes of passersby, hoping for the clink of change.

"If you wish to hear the remainder and loveliest part of the song, ladies and gentlemen, I leave it to your generosity to contribute a little more," Wiggins told the morning strollers. "There is the hat. Don't be afraid of throwin' in your money. I shall not be afraid of pickin' it up."

The morning was cool and gray, with a fine mist slowly soaking the cobblestones. Ozzie shivered in his thin coat and coughed again. With the coughs sometimes came a farthing or a half farthing or, if they were lucky, a halfpenny in response. The city folk seemed to appreciate Ozzie's asthma more than Wiggins's singing.

The boys had positioned themselves across the street and a few doors down from 221 B Baker Street, the address of their frequent employer, the world-famous consulting detective Mr. Sherlock Holmes. Holmes often contracted Wiggins and the rest of his gang to work on his most difficult cases. He called them the Baker Street Irregulars, and said they were "his eyes and ears on the street."

Wiggins stopped singing and crouched down to inspect the bowler. He counted three cents in all. "I wish Master would send for us. This crowd don't appreciate a true vocal artist." He swiped his wild, cider-colored curls from where they'd fallen in front of his face and looked up at the second-story windows of 221 B.

Ozzie followed his gaze. Since he'd been part of the Baker Street Irregulars for only a few months, he hadn't yet met Sherlock Holmes, but he had already worked on a couple of his cases. He knew quite a bit about Master from Wiggins and the other boys. For example, his detection skills were so sharp, they seemed almost like magic. But Master used only the facts in his methods, something Ozzie was learning to do, too. He was eager to meet Holmes. Maybe he would see some promise in Ozzie and put him on his payroll permanently. Maybe then he could leave his apprenticeship at the scrivener's shop, even save up enough money to go in search of the one thing he wanted most. Right-o, Ozzie said to himself, shaking off the dream.

Turning back to Wiggins, he said, "I think you look a bit too healthy, my friend, for us to benefit from the sympathy of strangers." Ozzie began another coughing fit, which resulted in a whole penny being tossed their way. Seeing the coin, the boys smiled.

"Healthy? Maybe next to you . . ." Wiggins patted his ample belly.

Ozzie looked at his friend, grinning happily, his hazel eyes shining like the coins in the bowler. When they'd first met, Ozzie had been walking aimlessly along the Thames, just days after his mother died. Wiggins invited him to share his fire. He'd even offered him some food, saying, "You're skinnier than me left leg, mate. And your skin's so pale, I believe I can see your veins. D'you know you've got blue patches 'neath your eyes?"

Ozzie remembered feeling self-conscious about the effects of all his crying, but even without it, his fair, almost translucent skin made him prone to sunken-looking eyes, especially when he slipped into one of his dark moods and lost sleep. His mum told him the blue patches were just the glow from his deep-set, sapphire eyes. "You're as handsome as my very own Sir Henry Irving, with the bearing of a fine stage actor as well," she used to say.

"Right," Ozzie had said to Wiggins, swallowing back the memory. "I suppose I could use a bit of food." Then, warmed by the fire, the boiled oats, and Wiggins's matter-of-fact kindness, Ozzie found himself blurting out that his mum had died.

Wiggins didn't say anything, but he handed Ozzie a tin cup filled with hot tea.

It wasn't long after that that Ozzie joined the Irregulars. Not all the boys were happy to have him — mostly, Ozzie realized, because it meant one more bloke sharing the food. But Wiggins had insisted, and when a few of the boys groaned, he said firmly, "This mate needs a place. He's recently lost his mum. Now some of you don't remember your folks, but some of you know what that feels like, so you should take pity on 'im."

Here Wiggins paused as some of the boys nodded in silent understanding.

In truth, Ozzie didn't want their pity. But he was glad to have a place to go besides the scrivener's shop. And the company of some mates might be nice, too. Ozzie never did have many friends, in part because he wasn't able to chase after them or play other games requiring too much physical exertion — his lungs being weak since he was a baby.

"Besides," Wiggins had continued, "this chum's clever, and you can see he don't eat much anyway."

Ozzie could see the boys' faces relax, and the littlest one, Alfie, had even run up to him, saying, "Sorry 'bout your mum. Me mum was a beautiful lady before she got dead from the croup."

Ozzie was taken aback by the openness and had patted Alfie's head awkwardly.

"It is settled then. We have a new member of the gang," Wiggins declared, and the boys all thumped their right fists on their chests twice to show they were in agreement.

With that, Wiggins had them all go around and tell their tales.

"I'll start, boys," he offered. "I never knew me parents, Oz. I was what you'd call a foundling, fostered by strangers till I was four years – or thereabouts, since I don't rightly know me birth date. Then I was on me own to scrounge for food and find warm places to sleep. The sewers wasn't half bad. I can't remember much of me childhood, except for cold baths in the Thames and a painful hunger in me belly." Wiggins's face clouded over as a faraway look glazed his eyes. He shook it off. "But all that's ancient history, now that I got the gang and these fine lodgings." He swept his arm in a semicircle.

After a momentary silence, he gestured toward the next boy.

As Ozzie listened to Rohan, Elliot, Alfie, Simpson, Fletcher, Barnaby, James, Pete, and Shem tell their stories, he learned that some had run away from orphanages, while others had lost their families more recently — from disease or fire, factory accidents or starvation.

Wiggins watched Ozzie's face flush with empathy. He'd seen the look before on boys when they'd first joined the gang. And Wiggins knew immediately that Ozzie felt the bond.

"What about you, mate? What happened to your da?" Elliot asked.

Ozzie had just stared blankly, all the questions he had about his father swirling around, making his head feel cottony and dull.

Wiggins had looked at him thoughtfully. "It's all right, mate. You're among friends now."

But still, Ozzie couldn't find the words to answer. What *had* happened to his father?

Thankfully, even though Elliot pressed on, Wiggins finally said, "You're not in your right mind. You can tell us another time."

Ozzie had nodded, hoping the question would be forgotten.

"Well, I'm a growin' boy, and I need food," Wiggins said now. At the mention of food, Wiggins's ferret, Shirley, poked her head out from his shirt pocket. He scratched beneath her chin. "Aye, Shirley, you won't have to catch me breakfast this morn'."

"And it's a right good thing," Ozzie said. The last time Wiggins had roasted one of Shirley's catches and prepared it for the boys, Ozzie had spent the night curled over a bucket.

Wiggins could see Ozzie's face turn a bit green. "Sorry, mate, didn't mean to remind you of the roasted Rat. That sure was a lot of vom —"

Ozzie waved Wiggins off. When he got on a tear about something, he could go for hours. And just hearing the word *vomit* would be enough to make Ozzie's stomach heave.

As the boys spoke, a grand four-horse coach trotted up

the street and came to a stop in front of 221 B. Wiggins pocketed the change, Ozzie popped the bowler on his head, and the boys ran over to see who was inside.

The driver of the coach wore a fancy coat and had powdered hair. Beside him the footman, similarly attired, sat with a rigid upright posture. When he jumped down to open the door, two more men stepped from the carriage. One was middle-aged and bearded, with a thick, athletic build. The other was quite young, with slicked-back hair and a square face. Both men were dressed immaculately in silk top hats, sharp white collars, and dapper gray wool coats. They entered the door to 221 B with urgency.

"Wish we knew what was goin' on in there," Wiggins said. "I hope it means some work for us."

Ozzie studied the crest on the coach door. His brow wrinkled the way it sometimes did when he was trying to piece together facts. "I believe we just saw the Prince of Wales."

Wiggins let out a long whistle. "Well then, we may have treasure comin' our way, mate!"

"If I am right, Master will not merely be consulted today," said Ozzie. "He will be engaged. And if he needs search or surveillance, we are as good as employed."

The boys looked back up at the windows to the study where Holmes was meeting with his guests. Now and again they would glimpse Master's tall, thin frame passing by the draperies.

"What do you think the prince wants with Master?" Wiggins asked.

"It must be a delicate matter," said Ozzie, "for the prince to appear personally, with no entourage."

"Maybe someone nicked the crown jewels and we'll 'ave to find 'em." Wiggins looked up at the coachman. "You got a guinea for me and me china plate?" he said, slinging an arm around Ozzie. The driver ignored Wiggins and continued speaking to the footman next to him.

Ozzie laughed. "Always going for the bees 'n' honey."

Wiggins grinned and punched Ozzie on the shoulder. "Now yer startin' to sound like one of us Irregulars, like you was born right beneath Bow Bells."

The boys began to wrestle. Though Ozzie was rail thin, he was nearly a head taller than Wiggins and had a sense of leverage. When Ozzie accidentally leaned a sharp kneecap on Wiggins's shirt pocket, Shirley squealed and darted out. The boys stopped wrestling and gave chase down the street.

Just before the next corner, Wiggins dove and caught her. Ozzie bent over, wheezing from the exertion.

Wiggins tucked Shirley back in his pocket. "Sorry for the squeeze, me girl." Then turning toward Ozzie, he asked, "You all right, mate?"

Ozzie nodded, but he remained bent over with his hands on his knees. He was making little whistling sounds as he struggled to breathe.

Wiggins put a hand on his back. "You need me to go get the cod-liver oil?"

Ozzie shook his head. "I'll be all right," he managed, and stood up a little straighter.

"Hey, Oz, look over there." Wiggins pointed toward the prince's coach. The prince, his assistant, Sherlock Holmes, and Dr. Watson had exited 221 B and were climbing inside. The footman closed the door behind them and hopped back up as the driver snapped the reins.

In a moment, the prince's carriage clopped past the boys.

"You up for stealin' a ride, mate?"

Ozzie grinned. "I was thinking the exact thing. I should get back to the shop or Crumbly will clobber me, but this seems worth a beating." Scanning the street, Ozzie noticed a two-horse cart heading in the same direction as the royal carriage. He nodded toward it. "Here comes our chariot!"

Wiggins let out a whoop as the boys hopped on the back and made off down Baker Street in pursuit of the prince. The coins they'd collected jangled in Wiggins's pocket like a song.

CHAPTER THREE
A feast in the Castle

When Ozzie and Wiggins returned, forty-five minutes later, to the abandoned carriage factory just off Baker Street — which the Irregulars referred to as the Castle — the boys were waiting for them.

As usual, Ozzie and Wiggins had entered the hideout through a small trapdoor on the alley side of the building (the front doors to the factory having long been sealed). They strode into the main workshop area with Wiggins whistling a happy tune.

Rohan greeted them from his post on the stately but dilapidated coach resting on blocks near the front of the room. He was a quiet boy with black hair and dark, gentle eyes. He'd inherited his grandfather's impressive height and his mother's calm temperament and was, in his father's words, "the pride of the Punjabi family," a memory that sometimes caused Rohan shame.

He knew his father had hoped to see him one day apprenticed to a barrister, not collecting refuse or begging for coins or idling away hot afternoons splashing in the fountains in Trafalgar Square with the gang. But those dreams had vanished a year ago into the sea, along with Rohan's father and his fishing boat.

At least Rohan felt useful to the Irregulars. Wiggins relied on him to keep them from getting into too much trouble while he was away. It was especially important that they not cause a ruckus during business hours, when they were most likely to arouse suspicion from the authorities. None of the boys wanted to end up in the workhouse.

"All is well, Punjabi?" Wiggins asked. He carried a small sack of potatoes that he and Ozzie had purchased with the change they'd collected earlier.

Rohan nodded and motioned to the boys, who were shooting marbles or whittling sticks.

Seeing Wiggins's sack, Alfie came running. "What do you mates got there?" He was the baby of the gang, with silver-white hair like a swan's wing and eyes the color of fresh honey. His ears resembled two large biscuits glued to the sides of his head, a condition which invited all manner of nicknames.

"Stones, Elf," said Wiggins, "to build with."

"Come on, I know you've some food there," Alfie complained.

They walked across to the center of the room where a stone fire pit glowed. A few boys whittled near the coals to keep warm. Others lounged on the second-story balcony that ran along the perimeter of the rectangular space.

Around the boys, strewn here and there throughout the workshop area, were a variety of found or stolen items: a collection of holey woolen blankets bearing dismal stains, a few limp pillows, decks of cards, a cannonball, a trunk with a missing top, half a cricket bat, horseshoes, a human skull, coverless books and magazines, a chipped teapot, empty milk cans, an anchor, a rat's tail, a pile of coal, a pair of rusted handcuffs, rope, and a can of grease. On the wall nearest the coach hung a faded print of Her Majesty Queen Victoria, and beside it, a chore wheel for Sundays, when Wiggins insisted they tidy up the place. As the leader of the gang, he felt he had to maintain certain standards.

"Man your sticks, boys, we have breakfast and a tale to tell," Wiggins sang, pulling open the sack. "Rosebuds for me pride and joys."

More boys, nine in all, joined the ring around the fire pit. Ozzie and Wiggins handed a potato to each. Rohan threw more wood on the fire, and the flames swelled. The boys pulled out their custom cooking sticks. Some were carved with patterns, others had handles wrapped with canvas or strips of leather. Wiggins's was a gilded fireplace poker, Ozzie's a thin bent wire with a small wood handle.

The boys skewered their potatoes, but Wiggins knew better than to bring up business until everyone had settled down and was cooking happily. When the comforting earthy smell of warm food filled the carriage factory, he started his tale. "This early morn', while the rest of you layabouts was dreamin' of chocolates and featherbeds, me and me mate Osgood 'ere were out scroungin' up some change." Wiggins held up his potato and inspected it before plunging it back into the flames.

"And guess who drives up to Master's flat? None other than the Prince of Wales himself, lookin' smart!" Wiggins had the boys' attention and he knew it, so as usual he strung out the story.

Since Ozzie already knew what happened, he only half listened. The other half of his mind began to wander, as it frequently did, to the same subject. Maybe his father was in the government, he dreamed, maybe he knew the prince.

Wiggins continued, "So they all get into the prince's carriage and me and Oz steal ride after ride, gliding from cart to coach, as graceful as . . . as . . . as sparrows. Now we've all stolen rides, but we were lucky and swift. The prince had four champion thoroughbreds pullin' his carriage, and we followed right behind 'em, all the way to Buckingham Palace."

"You met the queen?" Alfie blurted, spraying half-cooked potato from his mouth.

"Nearly. We followed right up to the gate and saw 'em ride in."

Or maybe, Ozzie thought, Father was in the army and guarded the palace.

"As soon as the coach pulled through the gates, Master jumped out and began walkin' to the right side of the palace, with the prince, Watson, and the assistant followin'. Master and the rest looked up at the windows, not pointin', just casual like. Then the next thing you know, Master is examinin' the ground, walkin' like he got a stuck neck."

Wiggins stopped and blew on his potato to cool it. He tried breaking off a piece, but it was too hot.

The boys began to yell.

"Come on, Wiggins!"

"Tell the tale!"

"Get on with what happened!"

Wiggins looked up. "Ah, well, they went back 'round and entered the palace. We waited awhile, and when they didn't come out, we left."

"That's it?" Elliot said. He was a doughy boy with a pasty complexion that matched the anemic London sky. His mop of red hair, faded blue eyes, and plump, turned-down lips betrayed his Irish roots. "All that and nothin' happened? Bugger all."

The other boys laughed.

"It means that Master has been engaged on a big case and he'll need us soon," Ozzie said, watching the steam rise from his potato. He tried to feel kindly toward Elliot. He'd lost his whole family when a fire burned down their cottage, and he had tried, without luck, to save the baby. But Elliot's poor disposition did little to engender sympathy.

"It means we'll be workin' for the royal family, Stitch," Wiggins added.

Elliot came from a family of tailors back in Dingle, on the west coast of Ireland, and he had a knack for sewing up just about anything — clothing for the gang, moccasins made from leather they'd found lying about the shop, even a bad cut, which earned him his nickname. That and the scar on his left cheekbone, which he claimed he got when he beat up six Surrey roughs. He said he had sewn up the cut himself, too.

When the boys finished cooking their potatoes, they moved to a large rectangle alongside the fire pit, scratched out with a stick in the dirt. The rectangle was divided into six smaller rectangles.

The boys settled in, and Alfie inspected his position on the floor. "Which room is it you eat in again?"

"…Master has been engaged on a big case and he'll need us soon."

"The scullery," Fletcher said.

"You idiot, it's the parlor," said Shem.

Ozzie swallowed a bite of his potato. "Servants eat in the scullery. And the parlor is for card playing, smoking, and entertaining. Proper folk dine in the kitchen or the dining room. Alfie, it looks like you're in the water closet."

The other boys laughed. "Elf's in the bog!"

Alfie quickly scooted out of the bathroom and into the dining room. "You can tease if you like, but I knows how to eat like a gentleman." Alfie waved the last chunk of his potato in the air, puffed his chest, and nodded toward the print of the queen on the wall.

The other boys laughed again, but a few of them inched their way over to the dining room, elbowing one another for space.

Meanwhile, Ozzie climbed up into the coach and rummaged through the front compartment until he came up with his bottle of cod-liver oil. He held it up to the light and noticed that the bottle was nearly empty. "You should have a dose each morning," his mother used to say. "It is good for your lungs." Ozzie took a swig and grimaced. He wondered if his father suffered from asthma. Mother always said she would share more about him when Ozzie was older. Well, he was nearly twelve years old now, but it was too late. How would he ever find him?

Besides having little means to search for his father, he had only one flimsy clue with which to begin looking. And his time was not his own. He was lucky to steal some hours each day with the gang.

"Tell me again what the palace looks like?" Ozzie heard Alfie ask, but his thoughts had begun to slip backward in time. Ozzie knew his mother had all good intentions in securing him a position as a scrivener's apprentice. Before her death, she paid his boss, Crumbly, with what little money she had, to care for and train Ozzie. Ozzie recalled vividly the meeting in Crumbly's office where it was all decided. Julia Manning wore her best dress, which hung loosely on her wasted frame. Crumbly appeared sober and relatively respectable.

"Though I am a humble businessman, Mrs. Manning, I have a reputation in my field. Oxford Scriveners are known far and wide for the copy services we provide. Since I have no nippers of my own, I have no one to pass all of this on to.

You never know how far your son may go," he said, flashing his bad teeth and poking the air with his stubby fingers.

Ozzie's mother had not been well enough to inquire about Crumbly's reputation. Instead she coughed violently into a handkerchief and asked Ozzie to leave the room so that she and the scrivener could speak privately. Ozzie never found out what they discussed, but weeks later when his mother died, Crumbly appeared in their dingy flat with a contract signed by her and took him away.

Instead of care, Ozzie received a pallet covered with a few potato sacks to sleep on, a bowl of gruel each evening, and more cursing and beatings than even the worst apprentice deserved.

The memory of Ozzie's first weeks with Crumbly still burned a hole in his stomach. Crumbly had him clean filth from the cellar and the water closet with his bare hands. When business was slow, Crumbly drank, and he was meaner with liquor inside him. In addition to hitting Ozzie for no reason, he locked him in the storage room and often forgot that he was there. Once it took two days before he came to fetch him.

But when Crumbly discovered that Ozzie possessed an extraordinary talent for copying documents, he eased up a bit and allowed him to leave the premises for short periods if there was no business or chores. After, of course, making it clear that Ozzie would be hunted down like an animal if he ran off.

It was on one of his first trips out that he met Wiggins.

"The palace is grand, mate," Wiggins answered Alfie. "With big gates and guards in uniform. The whole place seems to sparkle with riches. When Master summons us, who knows, we may be invited inside." Wiggins got up and practiced how he would bow before the queen.

Ozzie couldn't help but smile at his friend. He loved the way Wiggins approached everything with a bright spirit. Even when the boys were cold and bored and starving, he always assured them that things would turn out all right. Ozzie wished he had half Wiggins's optimism.

From inside his coat pocket, Ozzie pulled out the letter that might help him locate his father. In the past three months, Ozzie had posted the same letter five times to his dead grandfather's sister, Great-aunt Agatha, hoping she would remember him and have some information about his father's whereabouts. But Ozzie wasn't even sure what county Great-aunt Agatha lived in or, for that matter, whether she still lived. Five times the letter had been returned.

He tucked the letter neatly into a fresh envelope and readdressed it, this time to Wroxton. He then slipped it back into his coat pocket to post later.

Ozzie climbed forlornly into the driver's seat and picked up a tattered copy of *Beeton's Christmas Annual.* A pang of longing pierced his chest as he recalled his reading lessons with Grandfather, when they would travel together into the worlds of King Arthur and Odysseus and Aristotle. Ozzie could picture Grandfather nodding his schoolmasterly approval when Ozzie took the time to properly pronounce a difficult word like *maelstrom.*

"Go on and read us the story, Oz," Wiggins said good-naturedly, prodding Ozzie out of his reminiscence.

Ozzie tipped his head to Wiggins and paged through the magazine to the story called "A Study in Scarlet." It was about the murder of an American named Enoch Drebber and was the first story Watson had published about Sherlock Holmes.

"Yeah, read the part about us," Alfie said, "where Master sez we 'go everywhere, see everything, overhear everyone.' And 'ow we're better than the bloody Yard."

"I wish Master would send for us already. I'd rather get paid than risk the workhouse by beggin'." Wiggins broke off a piece of potato and ate it. Then he broke off another and fed it to Shirley.

The other boys grew quiet at the mention of the workhouse. Several of them had experienced the draconian institution, where children (and grown-ups) worked like slaves, often to their deaths, for no money, little food, and prisonlike accommodations. The boys who'd been inside had been lucky to escape with their lives, except Alistair, who'd been caught stealing a loaf of bread and was still locked up.

Elliot broke the momentary silence. "Nah, Ozzie, read the part about Wiggins."

The rest of the boys started chanting, "Wiggins, Wiggins, Wiggins . . ."

Wiggins looked upset for a minute and then laughed,

too. Elliot was referring to the part of the story where Watson first met him. "Go on, Oz. It's all right."

Reluctantly, Ozzie obliged: "'The spokesman . . . young Wiggins, introduced his insignificant and unsavory person.'"

"That git Watson hasn't solved a single case," Alfie protested.

"It's a mystery why Master keeps him for a partner," Rohan agreed.

"Our detective work makes Watson look bad. That must be why he won't write more about us in the stories," Wiggins said.

"Plus, he's likely envious that Master needs us. As far as I can tell, Master doesn't even take Watson on his big cases because he can't keep a secret," Ozzie reasoned. He turned back to the magazine and was about to continue reading where he'd left off yesterday when suddenly there was a knock at the trapdoor. The Irregulars froze, and Ozzie put down the magazine.

The knock came again, and with it a fierce whisper.

"Wiggins, open up!"

They all recognized Billy's voice.

Wiggins went to the door and let in Sherlock Holmes's page.

"Mr. Holmes needs to see you right away," Billy told Wiggins urgently. He wore a blue bellboy's cap and, as he spoke, his fingers worried the brass buttons on his blue wool coat.

"He is ready for us to meet the queen now, is he?" Wiggins asked, his eyes gleaming in the lamplight.

Billy shook his head. "Don't know how you learned about that, but this has to do with somethin' else."

Wiggins turned to Ozzie. "It's your chance to meet him, mate."

"If I don't get back to the shop, you know Crumbly will send the police after me. Find me later."

Wiggins nodded and, along with half a dozen other Irregulars, followed Billy to the door.

"Imagine Mr. Holmes gettin' inside the royal palace," Wiggins marveled.

"Yes," Billy said, "but what's funny is now he wants to go to the circus."

CHAPTER FOUR
A meeting at 221 B Baker Street

Though it was still morning, the skies had darkened and the fine mist had settled into a steady rain. The Irregulars left the carriage factory at a run with Billy barely managing to keep up. The streets exhaled a distinctly putrid smell, of sewage and soot ribboned with horse manure.

As Wiggins turned onto Baker Street, he collided with a police officer and sent him flying facedown into the street. Wiggins stopped. "Sorry, sir. I —"

The officer lifted his face from the mud and glowered.

Before he could get back on his feet, Wiggins yelled, "I've clocked a plod, chase the sun!" Then he tore down Baker Street, a few paces behind the rest of the boys.

With a collective howl, they sped through the street, weaving in and out of people, carts, and buggies. The splattered officer gave chase, blowing a mud-clogged whistle. The Irregulars ran straight to 221 B and, without ringing the bell, pushed open the front door and charged straight up the steps. In a heap, they tumbled through the door of the flat and into the sitting room.

Watson, startled by the ruckus, spilled a cup of tea onto his lap. "Ohhhh!" he yelped.

Across the room, Holmes sat calmly on his couch, smoking a clay pipe. His demeanor was so relaxed that he seemed to the boys to be in a slight trance. "I thought we agreed, Wiggins, that only you were to appear in my accommodations," Holmes said, studying the group, water dripping down their faces. Then, turning his attention to Watson for a moment, "Are you all right, my friend? You must be; you've been sipping that tea for half the morning."

Watson dabbed at his wet trousers with a cloth and muttered that he was fine.

Holmes returned his gaze to the Irregulars. "It appears from the sound of police department–issued boots coming up my steps that you boys are being pursued by the law. Please come in, Officer Grey."

The mud-covered bobby entered the room, breathing

heavily, his tall helmet tilted over his eyes. "Don't worry . . . Mr. Holmes . . . I will run 'em all out of 'ere and straight to the workhouse, the little band of thieves."

Mr. Holmes's landlady, Mrs. Hudson, appeared from behind the officer and studied the boys in silent disapproval.

"Take those urchins out of here!" Watson yelled, climbing out of his chair and laying the wet cloth on the table in disgust.

"Gentlemen, please, these boys, though ragtag, are part of my organization. Officer Grey, you certainly are not accusing them of a crime, are you? It appears from your muddied uniform that you have had an unfortunate accident. Which of you boys has run into the officer? Speak up."

Wiggins raised his hand.

"Of course, Wiggins, leading the pack as always."

Wiggins blushed. A few of the other boys began to jeer.

"Enough, enough," Holmes said. "Officer Grey, I am afraid that this whole incident is my fault. I summoned the boys, and they were responding to my call when the accident occurred. To remedy the trouble we have caused you, may I offer the services of my landlady, Mrs. Hudson? I am sure she would be happy to help clean your uniform. I imagine she may fix you an early lunch as well. Mrs. Hudson, if you wouldn't mind."

Mrs. Hudson gave Holmes a flustered look. "Mr. Holmes, really. Follow me, Officer." She waved to Grey, who pushed his helmet back on his head, glanced at the boys disdainfully, and stomped out.

"Right. Now, all of you, 'tention."

The Irregulars lined up, standing with hands at their sides and chins forward. Holmes walked down the line of boys, inspecting them.

"Still rat catching, Wiggins."

"Only when business for you is slow, sir."

"I thought I saw that ferret of yours moving around under your coat.

"And you, small one, mud larking can be dangerous, even when the tide is out. Be careful walking in the Thames." Holmes pointed to the mud lines above Alfie's ankles.

Alfie's eyes went wide, then blinked uncontrollably as he blurted out, "Eeeeyyes."

Holmes continued down the line of boys and stopped in

front of Rohan. "I don't believe I've seen you before, lad. Bengali?"

"East End," Rohan replied.

"First generation then," Holmes continued.

"Yes, sir. Me mum and dad was born in Calcutta — but they're dead now," Rohan answered with uncharacteristic verbosity. He didn't know why, but something about Master made him want to talk.

Holmes nodded a silent acknowledgment and then looked at Elliot. "And you must be the tailor who keeps all these boys in their breeches."

"How'd you know that?" Elliot asked.

"The calluses on the thumb and forefinger of your right hand and the squint lines at your eye creases are all characteristics of a tailor. There is also your colorful attire." He nodded to Elliot's fine coat and trousers, made from patched squares stitched together. "And, of course, someone has sewn all these moccasins, apparently from a single hide." Holmes nodded matter-of-factly at the boys' feet. Then he continued down the line. "So, Watson, what do you think of the troops?"

Watson raised his brow, twitched his mustache, and said with a pained expression, "With troops like these, we would have lost India long ago."

"I don't agree," Holmes said smartly, turning back to the boys. He gave a sharp double clap of his hands. "Now to business. Today, your job, I am sure, will have more than some appeal to you all. You are to conduct a surveillance of a circus. You must use your eyes, but also your ears."

Holmes picked up a newspaper off the couch. "'Last night at approximately eight thirty P.M. the world-renowned tightrope team, the Amazing Zalindas, fell to their deaths while performing in the main tent of the Grand Barboza Circus. Though the incident is being investigated by the police, the three deaths are thought to be a tragic accident — one of the most horrific ever reported in the history of show business — caused by a Faulty rope that snapped,'" Holmes read. "I believe there may be something more afoot."

Holmes handed the paper to Wiggins and started pacing. "You are to survey the Grand Barboza, mix with the performers, and learn what they say about the unfortunate Zalindas. Observe and absorb. We do not have much time."

"There is an extra guinea for the one who brings me the biggest lead."

Commotion erupted in the flat as the Irregulars spoke of their assignment.

"The circus is on the outskirts of St. John's Wood. I have arranged transportation for you. Try to stay out of trouble and learn what you can. I will appear with Watson in due course. I do not want it known that you are my agents. Only Wiggins is to have contact with me on the grounds. Now, if I am not mistaken, I hear the cart pulling up beneath our window."

The boys ran to the window to see.

"Your usual salary of a shilling per day each plus expenses still applies. Here is a day's pay and some extra in advance for your expenses. Remember, this is work." Holmes filled Wiggins's palms with coins and waved him to disperse them among the Irregulars. "There is an extra guinea for the one who brings me the biggest lead."

The boys cheered as they stampeded out of the apartment and down the stairs. In the vestibule, Alfie kissed a weary Mrs. Hudson on the cheek. "I'm goin' to be a rich boy!" he shouted before following the others into the damp late morning air, where the tiniest wisp of sunlight beckoned like a promise.

CHAPTER FIVE
The Irregulars arrive at the Grand Barboza Circus

Q uit starin' at me, you dirty little creature." The driver of the cart looked over his shoulder at Elliot. Elliot flashed a dark smile, causing the driver to tuck the small leather money sack bobbing from his neck back inside his shirt. "Why that gentleman would arrange a ride for the likes of you . . . I must be mad takin' you lot around."

"He paid you, so stop complainin'," Elliot said with a laugh.

"Yeah," Alfie added.

"All right, that's it, all of you, off! You're all fur coats and no knickers. I don't need no nonsense from a bunch of beggars." The driver halted the cart. "Now!"

The boys scrambled off, and the driver turned the cart around and rode away.

"Nice work, Elliot, you really told him," said Barnaby.

"Now we've got to walk like common folk," said Pete.

Wiggins and Rohan exchanged an exasperated look as the boys continued by foot along the muddy road.

About a half hour later, the Grand Barboza Circus loomed in the distance like a small tent city. The main tent, made of gray canvas, was surrounded by two dozen or so smaller tents and a variety of stands, carts, and caravans. By day, the circus had a strange bleakness that night could usually hide, and all the boys felt uneasy as they approached.

The origins of the circus are not exactly clear. Some say it began in Hungary or Romania or maybe Scotland. The performers and laborers came from throughout the world, giving the Grand Barboza a foreign air.

"Now remember, mates, we're on Mr. Holmes's business, so there'll be no foolishness. We're investigators." Wiggins looked particularly at Elliot and Alfie.

"I'm all business," Alfie said, starting an uneven march.

Elliot glared back at Wiggins.

"So what's the plan?" Rohan asked, looking up at the main tent.

"All right, mates, choose a performer and chat 'em up. We've got to find out what they know about the Zalindas."

Wiggins scratched the back of his head. Then he scratched the back of Shirley's. He thought about the fact that Holmes considered him the leader of the Irregulars. It was true he looked after the boys, and they listened to him (he'd been on the street the longest). But when it came to working for Holmes, the truth was that since Ozzie joined the gang, Wiggins deferred to him on such matters. Try to think like Oz, he told himself.

The boys looked up at the banners trumpeting the various attractions. They boasted words the boys could not read, but the pictures told them all they needed to know: A strongman with biceps like barbells bent a metal bar over his head, and a dark-eyed woman in a red turban stared into a crystal ball. There was a man being shot in flames from a cannon, a tall man, a doll-sized woman, elephants, trapEze artists, a bearded person wearing a dress, a man throwing knives, clowns, and a man with his head in a lion's mouth.

Wiggins had an idea. "All right, mates, choose a performer and chat 'em up. We've got to find out what they know about the Zalindas. Time's a wastin'."

CHAPTER SIX
In which the Irregulars interview
the circus performers

The lions' lair, a large cage mounted on a four-wheel cart, loomed some four and a half feet in the air, exactly at Elliot's eye level. He marveled at the huge cats lying sleepily only a few feet away on the other side of the bars. If these cats were mine, I could get things. People would see me and my lions and be so scared they'd do as I said.

"Ex-xxcuse me, little bb-boy-oy, don't get too close to the ba-ba-bars." A slight, pale-faced man in work clothes appeared from under the rear of the cart.

"Just lookin'," Elliot said cautiously.

"Luk-luk-looking is f-f-fine if you du-du-don't get your face scratched off."

Elliot stepped back. "Aren't they trained?"

The man laughed. "You can train-nnn 'em, but they're still li-li-lions."

"They ever hurt you?"

"Naah, but I give 'em resp-p-pect, and they know me."

Elliot paused and looked at the trainer. "You know anything about those tightrope walkers?"

"Only that they weren't care-careful, and that they had been spend-d-ding time with an outsid-der, which is always bad-d-d luck."

"What do you mean?"

The trainer studied Elliot carefully before walking around to the back of the cart. "D-d-don't get too cl-lose to the b-b-bars."

Rohan searched for the strongman unsuccessfully. Since he was tall and strong, too, the others assumed he'd want to interview him. There's more to me than my size, he thought as he turned absentmindedly into a small tent.

"Who are you?" two voices said simultaneously.

Rohan looked up and saw two faces reflected in a mirror staring back at him. The faces were oval and fair-skinned with almond-shaped eyes. Pretty faces and identical, except for the makeup. One of them seemed whiter than the other, with black lips and black eyebrows that rose in sharp arches. The other had pale pink lips and rounded auburn eyebrows. They sat close to each other on a bench with their backs to him, applying makeup.

"Speak up, what's your business?" the two women said in unison.

"I'm sorry," Rohan said. "I wasn't watching my step, and . . ."

"You can't just walk in on people like that," said the woman with the black lips.

"He said he was sorry," said the other.

The women rose from the bench and turned around. Rohan froze. Before him were the faces of two pretty women on delicate necks attached to one single body, wearing a robe. Rohan counted: two arms, two legs, two heads.

"Don't stare, it's rude," said the right head with the black lips.

"Be nice, he's sweet, and so handsome," said the left.

"You're ridiculous. He's a raggedy Indian boy."

"I am Angelina," said the left head, "and this is my sister, Balina, the surly one. They call us the Jekyll and Hyde twins."

"I'm Rohan," Rohan told them.

"Now that you've made our acquaintance, you can go on

"I am Angelina," said the left head, "and this is my sister, Balina, the surly one. They call us the Jekyll and Hyde twins."

your way." Balina tried to turn back around, but Angelina remained facing Rohan, which caused the twins to lose their balance. Rohan stepped forward to steady them.

"Thank you, but we're fine." Angelina smiled.

"Don't touch us." Balina scowled.

"I should go." Rohan moved toward the doorway.

"The circus isn't open for another few hours. What are you going to do?" Angelina asked.

"He shouldn't even be here. I'm going to call one of the fellas to take care of him," Balina threatened.

"Balina, behave yourself. He's just a boy. Can we help you with anything?"

Rohan thought a moment. "No, miss, I'm just enjoying the circus. It's a sad thing what happened to the Zalindas, though. I always wanted to see them perform."

"It's horrible when accidents happen," said Angelina.

"Accidents, hah!" Balina rolled her eyes. "That knife thrower is no accident. The jealous drunkard was behind it."

"Quiet, Balina! Don't bother the boy with such gossip." Angelina turned back to Rohan and smiled. "Come visit us at the sideshow later. We'd be happy to see you again."

In an annex to the main tent, Wiggins stood next to a large cannon, wondering if he should have chosen a different performer.

"I said, how long have you been the human cannonball?" Wiggins shouted.

"I'm not a cannibal!"

The man he was talking to was almost completely bald except for a tuft of frizzy hair over each ear. He wore skin-tight black trousers with braces attached to them but no shirt, and he was quite Stocky.

"Can-non-balllll!" Wiggins enunciated.

"Oh! I see," the man yelled back. "I've been at it four years! The name's Clarence!"

Clarence waved to the men at the other end of the cannon, and they promptly cranked the cannon tube downward.

"Is it scary?"

"Hairy?" shouted Clarence. "That's rather a personal question. But, yes, I used to be, lad, until the flames singed it all off."

Wiggins wondered how such a silly man performed an act of great daring. "Were you friends with the Zalindas?"

"What?"

"The tightrope walkers!"

"Sorry to hear what happened to them! Sometimes I wonder if I should find me some nice safe work on the ground! Those clowns really have the prize jobs! Just some makeup, baggy trousers, a little dance around, and everyone's happy! For me it's always 'higher Clarence, faster Clarence, farther Clarence!' No one's ever satisfied!

"Excuse me, son, I have to check the inner wall of the cannon for ridges! Almost shaved the skin off my belly last month!" Clarence stuck his head into the tube, saying, "Smooth, smooth, ah, yes."

As Alfie wandered the fairgrounds, he could hardly believe that the fat, friendly woman he had just spoken to had a beard. She was pretty, too, in a strange sort of way. He would have liked to stay and talk to her, but she didn't know anything about the Zalindas.

Feeling cold, Alfie walked toward a fire burning in an open area just beyond some of the smaller tents.

Four men and two women sat around the fire. All but one

of them perched on crates, leaning forward toward the flames. The man standing was tall and bald with a pointy, black beard. By his gestures, he seemed to be arguing with some of the seated people. Alfie got down on all fours and crawled within hearing distance of the group, crouching behind a series of boxes.

The standing man was rubbing his bald head and saying, "It's a tremendous opportunity, I tell you. We can do both, you know we can. Barboza has already asked."

One of the men sitting said, "For God sakes, Indigo, the bodies of those poor souls aren't even cold yet. We can't accept."

One of the women said she agreed.

"I am all for respecting the dead, but we have to think about what is best for us and the circus. Barboza needs tight-rope walkers, and it makes sense that we fill in. Before I did trapeze work, I was trained on the tightrope. I can do it, and most of you can, too. Barboza said he would even pay us for doing both acts, double pay for the same night's work. We can call ourselves 'The Flying Joneses — Royal Family of the Air.'" He moved his hands before his eyes like he was setting the type for their new banner.

"Indigo, you're mad," said one of the men.

"I don't know; I like the sound of double pay," said another. "Barboza will hire replacements eventually, so we might as well take the job and get the money while we can. I'm with you, Indigo."

Soon they all were talking at once. Some agreed, some didn't, but it appeared that the one who had been standing, Indigo Jones, was satisfied that his family was beginning to see things his way.

He lifted his hand for silence. "I have always followed the will of our clan. Because of this, we have missed opportunities in the past. I have created this opportunity for us, and we *must* seize it. Otherwise, all my sacrifices are a waste."

Indigo raised both hands in a solemn motion to the group. "Let us not fall victim to our fears again."

Alfie struggled to understand this man, Indigo Jones, who spoke in a strange manner. But it sounded like he was practically confessing to the crime! Already tasting the butterscotch his guinea would buy him, Alfie ran to find the others.

CHAPTER SEVEN
Wiggins discovers
the murder weapon

A short distance from where the boys had stationed themselves with the various performers, Holmes and Watson spoke with the ringmaster, Mr. Barboza, in front of the main circus tent. Inspector Lestrade of Scotland Yard stood by as well.

Barboza's long, blond mustache and curly blond hair had grown limp, and his showman's outfit looked as though he'd slept in it.

"Mr. Holmes, were my performers victims of a crime?" He rolled his *r*'s in the back of his throat.

"Mr. Barboza, I need more data before I can draw my conclusions. Is it true that the scene of the Zalindas' fall has not been disturbed?"

"That is correct, sir. Inspector Lestrade has seen to that.

Only the bodies of the Zalindas have been moved. Can we still open tonight?" Barboza asked with some anxiety.

"I don't anticipate any delay once Mr. Holmes finishes his investigation," answered Lestrade matter-of-factly. "We do not view this as anything more than an unfortunate accident caused by a faulty rope. Mr. HolmeS just likes to exercise his theories. We are extending professional courtesy, nothing more."

"I appreciate the courtesy, Inspector. Let's proceed to the big top, gentlemen," Holmes said with some vigor, striding purposefully into the main tent.

Ozzie crawled out from his hiding spot under a nearby cart and shadowed Holmes. Fortunately, Ozzie's boss, Crumbly, had spent a few too many shillings at the pub the night before and was now passed out in his flat above the shop. This, Ozzie had learned from Frankie, the principal scrivener.

After sitting down at his table and copying papers for close to an hour, Ozzie nodded to Frankie and slipped out. Frankie gave a slight nod back, signaling that he would cover for Ozzie should Crumbly emerge from his stupor.

When Ozzie returned to the carriage factory, no one was there, but Wiggins had dropped off the newspaper with the story of the Zalindas, which Holmes had circled in charcoal. Ozzie promptly hopped on the back of a cart heading north to St. John's Wood.

Now, as he crept stealthily along the perimeter of the tent looking for hidden access inside, he felt an odd sensation, as if he was being watched. When he turned, he saw out of the corner of his eye a cloaked figure run away.

The floor of the big top consisted of two large rings, surrounded by stands for the patrons. Three support poles ran down the center of the tent. The tightrope had been strung between two of these poles and now dangled in two pieces, one along each support pole. Three brown spots in the sawdust, oddly forming a crooked letter *M*, were the only reminder of what had occurred the night before.

Ozzie managed to crawl under the tent bottom, behind a section of stands. He watched from a distance as Holmes scrambled up the footholds on one pole, about twenty feet in the air, and pulled out his magnifying glass to examine the end of the rope. When he finished, he scrambled down, climbed up the other pole, and examined the other rope end.

At the opposite side of the tent, Wiggins emerged from the annex. Ozzie spotted him walking toward Holmes. Swiftly, Ozzie intercepted him before he reached Holmes and pulled him back into the stands.

"How'd you find us so quickly?" Wiggins said.

"I stole a ride or two. What's going on?"

Wiggins explained the assignment and what the other boys had learned about the Zalindas' deaths.

"What about the prince? Did Master say anything about the goings-on at Buckingham Palace?"

Wiggins shook his head.

"Hmm," Ozzie said quietly. Though he didn't blame Wiggins for not asking Master about the prince, he was curious why Holmes would involve himself in the deaths of circus performers the day after he was consulted by the Crown.

Through slats in the stands, Ozzie and Wiggins watched Holmes climb down from the pole.

"Look at him. He's as excited as Alfie when he's got a mouthful of toffee," Ozzie said.

Like a bloodhound, Holmes was now on all fours, sifting through the sawdust on the floor of the tent. He started at the outer edge of the circle and crawled inward in a spiral motion.

"Wiggins, something is up."

Wiggins nodded in agreement. "I'll go see what's happening."

"Good. Then meet me outside."

As Ozzie lingered outside the big top waiting for Wiggins, the strange feeling came over him again. He looked around and then, down a corridor of tents and stands, he spied the same small cloaked figure facing his direction. Instinctively, he knew he was being watched. Maybe this person had something to hide, he noted.

Ozzie walked around one of the smaller tents, planning to circle behind whoever it was and surprise him. But after going a short way, he lost his sense of direction and stepped out right in front of the cloaked figure, who squealed and ran.

Ozzie gave chase, darting around the smaller tents and following the person right through a doorway. He was stopped in his tracks by a woman, with dark, penetrating eyes.

"Who enters, unannounced, into the tent of Madam Estrella?" The fortune-teller held her arms before her and stared at Ozzie so intensely he felt hypnotized.

"Speak now!"

Ozzie began to cough. Before he could catch his breath, someone spoke.

"It's my fault, Mamá. He was following me." Behind Madam Estrella, the cloaked figure dropped her hood, revealing the face of a girl Ozzie's age. She was olive-skinned, with large eyes the color of peeled grapes and long, straight black hair. A colorful silk kerchief framed her forehead, and when she removed her cape, Ozzie noticed that the lining was made of purple velvet. Beneath that, she was draped from shoulders to ankles in bright silk scarves. Heavy jeweled ornaments adorned her ears.

"Pilar, explain," Madam Estrella demanded, her eyes still focused on Ozzie.

"Well, Mamá, there are a bunch of boys wandering around the circus grounds, asking a lot of questions about the Zalindas. I think he's one of them. So I followed him, and well, he followed me." She spoke with an English accent, but the foreign flavor of her native tongue leaked through on certain words.

"An investigator," Madam Estrella said to Ozzie, holding back a smile. "Are you with Scotland Yard?" She was a big woman with an ample bosom, and she was clad in a shining velveteen caftan, spangled with buttons of gold, silver, and pearl. A bright red silk scarf covered her head, and enormous gold earrings dangled down her thick neck.

"I have just come to see the show," Ozzie said casually.

"The show doesn't start for hours," said Pilar.

"I didn't know that, but now that I am here, I've been watching the animals."

"There are no animals in the big top, just police," Pilar countered.

Madam Estrella raised her brow. "Where are your parents, young man?"

Ozzie had not expected to be cross-examined, and this last question, though the easiest to answer, threw him off balance. "They're not here," he said awkwardly.

Madam Estrella studied Ozzie carefully. "Would you like a reading?" she asked.

Wiggins had been assisting Holmes with the search when Alfie, ignoring Holmes's earlier instructions, ran up to him and held out an open hand. "If you don't mind, sir, I'd like me guinea."

Holmes considered the boy quizzically.

Alfie leaned in so the others wouldn't hear. "I've found the murderers," he whispered.

"Have you?" Holmes said sardonically. "Well then, a guinea awaits you after you help me find the murder weapon and prove my theory."

"Yes, but you said —"

"Now, boy!"

Alfie looked imploringly at Wiggins, who gave him an angry glare. Alfie dropped down and joined him in the sawdust.

Resuming his digging, Holmes warned the boys to be very careful, for the object in question was small but deadly. He scanned the sawdust intently, his eyes piercing, like a bird of prey.

Alfie crawled fast, kicking up sawdust like a hamster.

Watson, Barboza, and Lestrade stood watching them as if they were all mad.

Wiggins patted the sawdust lightly, wondering with a slight concern what they were looking for. He watched Holmes's deliberate movements and tried to emulate them, though his hands were thick and clumsy. Still, Wiggins felt proud to be working so closely with Holmes and excited about the feast he would cook up for the boys with their pay.

Wiggins's mind was thus engaged when he felt a sharp sting in his left hand. The pain shot a lightning bolt up his forearm. He yelled as he turned over his palm, which showed a long pinlike object projecting straight up from its center.

Before Wiggins could respond, Holmes grabbed his left wrist firmly, pulled out his magnifying glass, and examined the pin. Roughly the length of Holmes's forefinger, it looked like a thick needle, hollowed out at its center. A small razor nested inside it. Holmes muttered to himself aloud, "The craftsmanship of a genius." Then with a swift pull, he dislodged the pin from Wiggins's hand.

Wiggins winced and bit down on his lip to keep from crying out.

"Good job, my boy." Holmes gave Wiggins a light pat on the shoulder. "Watson, see if you can do anything for our friend here." Holmes motioned to the wound in Wiggins's palm, handed him a clean handkerchief to wipe the blood, and turned back to the pin.

With both hands, Holmes gave the device a forceful twist to close it and placed it in a small envelope he obtained from his vest pocket.

"Lestrade, you have a triple murder on your hands," Holmes said decisively.

"Murder! More theorizing, Mr. Holmes?" Lestrade folded his arms across his chest.

Alfie couldn't help but notice that the inspector's pointy face looked a bit like Shirley's.

"I have examined the ends of the rope myself," Lestrade continued, "and they are clearly frayed, showing that it snapped from tension, not from mischief."

"I am sure you have seen all there is to be seen, Lestrade; it is simply your inferences that miss the mark. Have your men lower the remnants of the tightrope to the ground, and in the meantime, Mr. Barboza, if you could answer a few questions."

"Let's begin with the date of your birth." Madam Estrella and Ozzie sat at a small round table with a crystal ball in the center. Pilar stood a few feet away, her arms scissored across her chest, watching impatiently.

"October tenth, 1877."

"It's almost your birthday," Pilar noted drily.

"*Cállate, hija* – hush, daughter. Give me your hands, young man."

Reluctantly, Ozzie did. Madam Estrella closed her eyes, tilted her head back, and rocked in her chair. She began to hum.

Ozzie was annoyed with himself. He should be gathering information for Master, not wasting time having his fortune told.

"I need you to keep your mind blank, young man, and to stop questioning my powers." Madam Estrella took hold of Ozzie's hands. She closed her eyes again and continued to hum. When she spoke, her voice was deep and hollow. "The coming year will be one of great challenges and triumphs. The spirits tell me that someone is watching over you. I see the figure of a man, but his face is not clear. I see puffs of small

"The spirits tell me that someone is watching over you."

clouds . . . but wait. Now I see shadows, and I hear a violin. A woman — fair, gentle, with chestnut hair, tied in a bun — she is smiling, she is trying to tell me something, but . . . but . . ."

"What?" Ozzie asked.

"She's coughing. She is waving, as if telling you to go away."

Ozzie's brow began to burn, and he tried to pull his hands away from Madam Estrella, but she held on with a firm grip. Was she really seeing his mother? He wanted to go, but now he needed to hear more. Mother and violin music? Did his father play the violin?

"Now I see an old woman in a rocker. She is rocking and pointing at you, saying, 'I know, I know.' I see another figure. He's tall and gaunt, and he's surrounded by sheets of ice. He carries something beneath his arm, a small door or a box with light seeping from its borders. The ice around him is melting, cascading. It's a torrent." Madam Estrella began to perspire. Ozzie felt her tremble. She gasped, then abruptly she looked up from the crystal ball and dropped Ozzie's hands. She mopped her forehead with her sleeve, which seemed to signal that the reading had ended.

"What is it?" Ozzie asked. "What did you see?"

Madam Estrella shook her head, as if unburdening herself of the vision.

"Tell me," Ozzie demanded, surprising himself.

"My daughter says you are seeking information about the Zalindas." Madam Estrella's voice was different now — casual, conversational.

Was the old woman Madam Estrella had seen Ozzie's great-aunt Agatha? Why wouldn't Madam Estrella tell him more? What could she have seen that was too terrible to relate?

"If the death of the Zalindas was more than an accident, you must consider those who benefited —" Madam Estrella began.

"The Joneses!" Pilar exclaimed.

"— and those who hated them." Madam Estrella frowned at Pilar. "The knife thrower, Karlov, despised the Zalindas."

"It was because of Penelope!" Pilar offered.

"Perhaps you would like to speak for me, *hija*," Madam Estrella said, slightly vexed.

"Well, Mamá, this part is just gossip. Everyone knows that Karlov's assistant, Penelope, ran off with the youngest brother, Cesar Zalinda, and that Karlov was in love with her and now he hates the Zalindas."

"Hated," said Ozzie. "They're dead, if you recall." Ozzie recognized that he would not get any more information. He was not entirely certain he could trust the information he had ascertained. And yet, it gnawed at him. He stood to leave. "Madam Estrella, I appreciate the . . . the —"

"Reading," Pilar said.

"Reading," Ozzie finished. "But I really must meet my mates."

"One more item, young man, and this is not gossip." Madam Estrella stood, put her hand on Ozzie's shoulder, and stared into his eyes. "You must beware of the stranger."

CHAPTER EIGHT
Holmes discloses the crime

Barboza was red in the face — from frustration or anger, one could not tell. He was not a man accustomed to answering questions. The more uncomfortable he became, the more his accent seemed to change from something of Eastern European origin to something with a more local flavor. "Mr. Holmes, the Zalindas were a good lot, affable chums who got on well with others. Only recently did they isolate themselves when they began to keep company with a fellow who claimed to be a rope salesman. I bought a few coils from him myself."

"Did he sell you this one?" Holmes asked, pointing to the torn tightrope that lay before them.

"No, sir, I know for a fact that we obtained that one from a different source. I oversaw the lads stringing it up yesterday.

What I *can* tell you is that the rope salesman spent quite some time with the Zalindas over the last fortnight. He seemed — well, this may sound odd, but — not right for his trade."

"Did the Zalindas have any enemies?" asked Watson, who until now had remained quiet.

"Enemies!" Barboza shouted, and then paused awkwardly. "I would say not. We are a family, sir, perhaps an unusual one, but a family nonetheless."

"The Joneses hated the Zalindas," Alfie blurted. "They wanted 'em dead."

"Who is this bounder?" Barboza demanded.

Wiggins shot Alfie a withering look and clapped his good hand over his mate's mouth.

"Never mind the boy. He suffers from an overactive imagination. Now, it is my understanding that three deaths occurred here, but that there were four Zalindas. Where is the fourth?" Holmes watched Barboza carefully for his response.

"I must say, Mr. Holmes, you have learned quite a bit about our little family. Yes, there were four Zalindas. The youngest was Cesar, a handsome and delicate boy. He disappeared with a girl who was an assistant to one of our performers about three days ago. No one, including the Zalindas themselves, knew where they went. It was a matter of the heart."

Lestrade interrupted. "All this is very nice, Mr. Holmes, but you have yet to show us evidence that there was any wrongdoing here."

"It is true, Holmes; you are keeping us in suspense," Watson added.

"Gentlemen, you are quite right. Let us begin with the rope that has been sabotaged." Holmes lifted one end of the rope.

Wiggins and Alfie moved closer to see.

"Clearly it's frayed, Holmes, which shows that it snapped from stress," Lestrade offered.

"Yes, it is frayed, Lestrade, but it is not simply a stress tear. I have made a formal study of hemp and its uses. In fact, I plan to write a monograph on the subject. This is the most cleverly cut rope I have ever seen, or read of, for that matter, including the case of the Cardiff hangman who spared his victims for the right price by adroitly slicing the noose in such a manner that it would snap only moments before his clients were asphyxiated." Holmes ran his hand over the frayed strands of rOpe.

"Pray, look at the rope in question. As Lestrade has so artfully pointed out, it is frayed, but see what happens if I slide the frayed ends back. Look at the center of the rope."

"It is smooth," observed Watson.

"As if freshly cut," said Wiggins.

"Exactly. Some ingenious villain sabotaged this rope by cutting out its center, so it would appear to the Zalindas – and anyone else – to be sound, when in fact the middle strands had been sliced, leaving the rope whole but hollow. Only after the weight of all three Zalindas had been placed on the rope for a sufficient period of time did it unravel and snap, creating the frayed strands. If you look at the end of the other length, it appears the same."

Lestrade's eyes grew wide. "But what device could make such a slice? It would have to cut the rope from the inside out."

"Brilliant, Lestrade, your insight overwhelms me." Holmes removed the envelope from his vest pocket and pulled out what appeared to be a large needle with one flat end.

Wiggins and Alfie craned their necks to see.

"Some ingenious villain sabotaged this rope by cutting out its center...."

"A needle, Holmes?" Watson said in disbelief.

"Not exactly." Holmes gave the needle a twist and slowly pulled the ends apart, revealing its razor center. Another twist, and the needle locked in the open position with the razor exposed. The length of the whole device was about three inches — the diameter of a large rope — a tightrope.

"Think of the skill that went into creating this small device, gentlemen. The thought and craft. Holding on to the flat end of this instrument, our murderer pushed the point into the rope; then with a slight twist and pull, he was able to open the razor and lock the device so the razor would remain open. With small back-and-forth motions, he sliced the internal strands of the rope without any damage to the exterior."

"But why leave it behind?" asked Wiggins and Watson at the same time.

"Ah, that's the trick. Even the most perfect device has its shortcomings. Once open and locked, this device cannot be closed without some leverage. Undoubtedly, after our villain completed his job, he could not close the instrument and remove it without slicing the rope clear through. He realized that by pushing the device completely into the rope, this small flat end would remain exposed, but as you see, it is no larger than a pencil tip. He knew it was unlikely to be discovered."

Barboza looked at Holmes with all pretension gone. "But why would anyone go to so much trouble for these three . . . ?"

"Mr. Barboza, or as I believe you were known before you went into show business, Mr. Abel Price, that's exactly what I must find out. Lestrade, I will contact you at the Yard this evening with what I have learned. By the way, Mr. Price, have you found a substitute act for the Zalindas?"

Barboza, or Price, in shocked awe, stammered, "Yes . . . the trapeze artists, the Flying Joneses, will now walk the rope."

"Very convenient," said Holmes. "Come, Watson, we must be off." Holmes looked to Wiggins and Alfie and, as he strode out of the tent, gave them a nod toward his carriage. They followed eagerly.

"See, I was right about the Joneses. Do I get me guinea now?" Alfie asked excitedly.

"I never!" said Watson.

"I didn't ask you, sir," said Alfie.

Wiggins put a hand on Alfie's shoulder and looked up at Holmes. "What would you like us to do next, Mr. Holmes?"

Holmes smiled. "Ah, Wiggins, always alert for the next command. Good lad. I trust your hand is improved."

Wiggins nodded, though in truth his palm was still throbbing.

"Right then. Focus your investigation on Karlov the knife thrower and the Flying Joneses," Holmes continued. "Our young blond friend may be on the way to earning his guinea yet. I plan to follow another line of investigation. I am interested in buying some rope."

CHAPTER NINE
The Irregulars meet Pilar

The Irregulars gathered by the carousel and were discussing their next step when Pilar approached. She waved to Ozzie and smiled, as though they'd arranged to meet at this very spot.

Ozzie cringed.

Alfie looked up and grimaced. "Who's she?" He'd been drawing a diagram of the circus grounds in the mud with his finger. "We're not lettin' girls in the gang, are we?"

"Girls are daft." Elliot coughed up a ball of mucus and spit. But he eyed Pilar's cape admiringly. He could sew himself a smart pair of trousers with such fine fabric.

Ozzie explained about Pilar.

"So these are your mates," she observed, coming closer and positioning herself between Ozzie and Wiggins, who was exactly her height.

"We're not lettin' girls in the gang, are we?"

Ozzie smiled weakly.

Wiggins leaned in front of Pilar toward Ozzie and mock whispered, "No time for chattin' up, Oz. We're workin' 'ere."

The others erupted in laughter.

Pilar ignored the boys and climbed confidently onto a pink-and-gold carousel horse in mid-gallop. She stroked its flowing mane. "I live here, and I know more about the circus than anybody. If you want to find out what happened to the Zalindas, you need me."

Somewhere in the distance an elephant trumpeted.

"We don't need anybody, thank you," Ozzie told her politely.

"From what I can see, you do." Pilar beamed a satisfied smile. When her lips turned up, her cheekbones kissed the creases of her eyes, making her look soft and fierce at the same time.

"Do you know who we are, girl? We're the Baker Street Irregulars." Wiggins paused, waiting for some Recognition.

Pilar looked at him blankly.

Wiggins puffed his chest. "We've been by chosen by

London's greatest detective, Mr. Sherlock Holmes, to work on his most difficult cases. It's dangerous work." He held up his bandaged hand.

Pilar was unimpressed. "Was that the man with the police? The tall, skinny one?"

Ozzie collected himself. "We're not answering any more questions. My associates and I have things to discuss. So if you wouldn't mind . . ."

"You're still here, so that means he wants you to investigate more. You must be considering Karlov and the Joneses." Pilar held the carousel post with one hand and tapped the forefinger of the other against her lips. Her gaze drifted off to the smaller tents clustered around the big top and, as she spoke, it was as much to herself as to the boys. "I can help you."

The boys began to groan and jeer. But Ozzie softened, thinking Pilar might be of use.

Wiggins noticed his friend's change of heart. "I know what, Oz, why don't you, Alfie, and the girlie go find the knife thrower, and the rest of us 'ere will go lookin' for the Joneses."

"Well, I . . ." Ozzie stammered.

"That's a good idea," said Pilar, hopping down from the carousel horse. "The Joneses will either be in their caravans across the way or in the big top practicing. Karlov is in his tent." Pilar pointed to each destination.

"I'm followin' the rest of you. I'm not goin' with no girl." Alfie crossed his arms in protest.

Pilar drummed her fingers on her elbows and let out an exaggerated sigh.

Wiggins thought for a moment. He knew Rohan could be trusted to look after the others and see to it that they stay focused on the investigation. "I'll go with you then, Oz," he offered. "Rohan, you and the gang go find the Joneses."

Rohan nodded his consent.

Before Wiggins could give further instructions, Pilar examined him and said, "Fine. Follow me. Karlov's tent is this way."

CHAPTER TEN

In which Pilar faces Karlov
the knife thrower

Ozzie and Wiggins matched Pilar's swift strides across the circus grounds as the rest of the boys hurried off with Rohan.

"Tell us about the knife thrower," Ozzie said.

"Karlov is a strange man with a bad temper. I don't like him. His assistant, Penelope, was beautiful. She was my friend. When I was little, she used to help me practice speaking English. In exchange, I taught her Spanish and Romani, the Gypsy language. Last year, for my tenth birthday, she made me this cape." Pilar lifted up the edges, studied them mournfully, then let go. "Karlov wanted to marry her, but she was much too young for him. Somehow she managed to resist his advances and keep working with him. I miss her." Pilar's voice broke up on this last bit.

Ozzie asked awkwardly, "So what happened to her?"

"Penelope and Cesar Zalinda had been spending time together. Penelope would only tell me a little, but it was easy to see she seemed different lately — happier. Karlov got suspicious and jealous. I saw him yelling at her one night, and then he tried to hit her. She and Cesar both disappeared three days ago, and no one's heard from them since. Karlov spends all his time alone in his tent now."

"Has he been performing?" Wiggins asked.

"Yes, but no one wants to assist him. So his act has been limited and not drawing the usual excitement from the crowd."

Ozzie hummed thoughtfully. "Perhaps we can use that."

"What do you mean, Oz?"

"The fact that Karlov needs an assistant is an excuse to speak with him. I could say I'm looking for work and volunteer to help him."

Wiggins nodded admiringly. "You always have a plan, Oz."

Pilar laughed. "Who ever heard of a knife thrower having a boy assistant?"

Ozzie and Wiggins were quiet. In truth, neither had ever seen a knife-throwing act and were unsure what an assistant even did.

As the three approached a medium-sized tent with a red satin curtain covering the doorway, Pilar paused. "I should do it. I can offer to assist him. He knows who I am, and he knows I sometimes assist my mother with her act. You two stay out here and listen. I'll try to keep him talking, and maybe he'll give something away."

"You're not an experienced investigator," said Ozzie. "You'll make him suspicious."

"If you move to the side of the tent, lift up the flap, and peer in, you can watch what's happening. I'll make sure he's facing the other way so he shouldn't notice."

Both boys motioned to stop her, but she had already pulled aside the curtain and stepped inside.

The rest of the gang had found the Joneses in the main tent.

"They're on the bloomin' tightrope. How we supposed to do our jobs with 'em up there?" Elliot was frustrated, a condition which caused his cheeks to flush and the tips of his ears to burn.

"We'll 'ave to wait," Rohan told him evenly.

Alfie sat on the ground beneath the stands with the others and let Shirley crawl up and down his shirtsleeves. Wiggins had put the ferret in his care for now. While wandering the grounds earlier, Alfie had seen a boy who'd trained canaries to ride in a little coach and walk a tightrope, and mice that could climb poles and carry down flags. Surely such an act would bring in lots of coins on the street, Alfie thought as Shirley skittered up his left arm, across his shoulders, and down the right. He planned to tell Wiggins to train her to perform her own circus act. Meanwhile, he and the gang waited beneath the stands in the main tent and watched the Joneses practicing theirs.

"Now remember, when we prove they're the guilty ones, I get me guinea," Alfie reminded everyone.

"If you hadn't already spent your shilling on the peep show, you mightn't be so greedy for the guinea," Elliot said. "The circus ain't even open yet, so you were robbed, payin' the shilling just to watch 'em practice."

Alfie ignored the logic of Elliot's statement and patted Shirley. "Yer just jealous you missed the show. It was about the *murder* of a woman. She was real pretty. They showed her before she died, lookin' so lovely on a swing in the garden. Then, after she was killed, her ghost appeared three nights in a row to her mum. It was the *ghost* what led them to the murderer!"

Rohan placed a hand on Alfie's head. "Hush, mate, or you'll give up our cover."

The rest of the Irregulars sat quietly, watching the Joneses walk the rope. The excitement of working at the circus had worn off, and now they were tired and hungry.

Flustered, Ozzie and Wiggins looked at each other and ran to the spot Pilar had suggested. They dropped down onto the straw and gently lifted the tent flap. Wiggins tried to clear a patch of ground around them. Straw nearly always brought on an attack of Ozzie's allergies or asthma.

The interior of the tent was extremely dark with only a single blue flame of lantern light. Strewn about the floor were empty alcohol bottles, crusty plates and bowls, cigar and biscuit boxes, and foul-smelling clothes. Open steamer trunks overflowed with strange, menacing objects: chains; a saw blade with angry teeth; long, spearlike rods; a cudgel; and a coil of rope.

Pilar's eyes were still adjusting to the dark when she saw

the spinning disk that Karlov used in his act. The disk was the size of a tall adult. Thick leather straps with ominous buckles dangled from it. Though Pilar had been in many circus tents, something about Karlov's made her shiver.

A rustling sound came from over by the cot. Pilar looked at the corner of the tent and, in the dim half-light, she watched Karlov swing his legs over the side and sit up with a groan. He rubbed his eyes and then gazed toward her.

Karlov turned up the light on the lantern, and Pilar felt herself rooted to her spot.

"Are you real?" he asked. "Or are you a bloody vision?"

About this time Pilar noticed, out of the corner of her eye, Ozzie and Wiggins poking their heads under the edge of the tent.

"It's me, Pilar," she said, gathering her courage.

Karlov's expression seemed unchanged. He waved. "Come closer."

Pilar took hesitant steps toward him.

"Fortune-teller's daughter, what do you want? Gyppos bring me bad luck."

Karlov struggled to his feet. The black bristle of his unshaven face, watery red eyes, and dirty black hair that stood up in stiff clumps suggested that he had taken to his bed. A large, dirty white shirt hugged his generous belly. He staggered to a nearby table and rummaged through the menagerie of objects on it. Empty bottles clinked.

"I'm sorry about Penelope. I miss her, too. She was a friend."

Karlov stopped. "What, what?" He stumbled toward Pilar, raising his fist and grabbing her around the neck by her cloak. "Do not speak that name to me, ever!" Karlov slurred and spit, his eyes inflamed.

Pilar's lungs felt as if they were collapsing, and she gasped for air.

Ozzie could feel a scratchiness developing at the back of his throat. He swallowed and took slow, steady breaths as he and Wiggins tried unsuccessfully to pull their bodies under the bottom edge of the tent to help Pilar.

Then, in a flicker, Karlov's mood changed. He spun away from Pilar, returned to the table, and rummaged some more. "Ahh," he sighed, lifting a small, flat bottle to his mouth. "The elixir."

Pilar rubbed her neck where the seam of her cloak had bitten into her skin.

He stumbled toward Pilar, raising his fist....

"Why have you come and disturbed me, child?" he grumbled mildly.

"I thought I could help you. I thought that you needed an assistant," Pilar offered with a slight quiver.

"An assistant!" he yelled. "She wants to replace my bloody assistant!"

Pilar stepped back.

Karlov lifted the bottle to his lips and swigged.

Pilar did not know what to do. She thought of leaving, for talking with Karlov seemed impossible.

By this time Wiggins had managed to lift up the bottom of the tent enough that the boys could crawl in if they had to, but they remained positioned as before. Ozzie felt his throat begin to constrict and, after every attempt to retain his breath, he finally coughed.

"What was that?" Karlov's gaze darted to the back end of the tent.

Wiggins dropped the flap he was holding and patted Ozzie on the back.

Ozzie coughed again.

"Blasted demons!" Karlov lifted the lantern and had stood to investigate when Pilar began to cough uncontrollably.

"Excuse me, sir," she said in between manufactured fits.

Karlov turned back toward Pilar and set down the lantern. "It's you. Bloody Gypsies are always spreading plague – the lot of you should be quarantined!"

"I'm better now. Mamá says I likely picked up something from the clowns."

Ozzie swallowed slowly and rubbed his throat with his hand. It quelled the coughing fit.

"I am sorry, my dear," Karlov continued. "As you can see, I am not myself these days and have a labile temper. I would be happy to give you an audition now." He flashed a tortured smile and stepped forward. Taking Pilar by the hand, he led her to the disk.

Karlov pulled over a small stool and instructed Pilar to step on it. He lifted her right arm, then buckled the leather strap around her wrist.

"Stay calm, my dear. That is the key." He lifted her left arm and buckled a strap around that wrist. "If you stay calm, people will never suspect that anything bad could happen to you. Now place your feet on the pegs." Pilar moved her feet from the stool onto two pegs that protruded from the lower portion of the disk.

Karlov bent over and tightened the leather strap around Pilar's right ankle. "Penelope was always calm and poised. That's why I never knew what she was really thinking." Karlov buckled the last strap around Pilar's left ankle. She was now strapped down, with her arms, legs, and head extended like a five-pointed star.

"Let's see how calm you can remain, shall we?" Karlov removed the stool and pulled a lever next to the disk.

Pilar knew the act. She had seen it before. But Karlov had such an entrancing effect on her that she only realized the danger of what she had volunteered to do as the disk slowly began to rotate.

Above the Irregulars' hiding spot, a figure climbed into the stands. The boys peered up through the slats to see a clown in full makeup, wearing a baggy suit with a large collar. He stood with his arm outstretched as if proffering a plate to be filled with food. "Let me see. 'Alas, poor Yorick! I knew him, Horatio, a fellow of infinite jest, of most excellent fancy; he hath bore me on his back a thousand times. . . . ' "

"Who's he talking to?" Alfie whispered loudly.

The other boys motioned to him to keep quiet.

Then a second clown with a floppy hat stepped into the stands. He carried two steaming cups in his hands and a tin of biscuits tucked under one arm. "Teatime in the big top, sir. Here's your cuppa. Who are you today? Romeo?"

"No, fool," said the one with the big collar, taking his cup, "I'm the Prince of Denmark."

Floppy Hat offered the tin of biscuits to his colleague. "Digestive?"

"Don't you wish for anything more serious or significant than playing the fool as you do each day?"

"Oh, I don't know. The crowd's always glad to see me, and the lads and lasses have a laugh."

"But, iMagine a life of real theater: tragedy, drama, and a mature audience!" Big Collar accepted a biscuit, then sipped his tea, gagged, and spit. "It tastes of soap!"

"It's herbs. You need to let it steep, that's all."

"Steep! You used soapy water to make the tea."

"I did not. I scooped it from the freshwater barrel."

"And where was the barrel?"

"Outside of the elephant tent," Floppy Hat said sheepishly.

"The elephant tent! How long have you been getting

water from there?" Big Collar dumped the tea on the ground and spit once again.

Below him, the boys dodged the liquid projectiles.

Big Collar bit into his biscuit.

Floppy Hat shrugged and took a sip. "Tastes fine to me."

"That's because you have the taste buds of a flea, you imbecile."

The painted smile on Floppy Hat's face drooped.

"Oh, please, Watty, don't go all weepy on me."

But it was too late. Fat tears slid down Floppy Hat's face, leaving tracks in his perfectly drawn cheeks.

"Oh, all right. I'm sorry. Now quit your blubbering," said Big Collar.

Floppy Hat promptly did and the clowns watched the Joneses on the tightrope, oblivious to the group of boys eavesdropping below them.

Meanwhile, Karlov staggered back to the table, untied a large leather bundle, and unrolled it. Twenty foot-long throwing knives lay sheaved in perfect symmetry. Pilar now spun on the disk at a second hand's time.

Karlov lifted his bottle and took another swig. Then he pulled a knife from the sheath and threw it. The knife stuck in the area immediately below Pilar's right arm. She stifled a yelp as Karlov took another swig. "You're remaining calm. Good," he said, and landed another knife just below her left shoulder.

Wiggins, who had lifted the tent bottom again, watched in horror as Karlov continued to drink whiskey and throw knives. "He's barmy. I'm goin' in after her, Oz," he whispered.

"Wait."

Wiggins looked over at Ozzie. He appeared to be scanning the tent. How could he focus on anything but this girl's life, especially with the wide look of fear now filling her eyes?

Without a word, Ozzie crawled stealthily into the tent, motioning for Wiggins to follow.

After throwing the third and fourth knives, Karlov walked back toward the disk. "You are doing well. Let us see how far we can go, shall we?" and he maniacally pulled the lever farther forward, causing the disk to spin faster and faster.

*   *   *

"That Indigo looks like he was born on the tightrope. He sure made a quick study of the art," Floppy Hat observed.

"I tell you, Indigo has the mark of the dark one on him, he does — that bald head and pointy beard, our own Mephistopheles. He seems a little too ready for the job, if you ask me, as though he'd known all along it would be his." Big Collar reached for another biscuit. "I've heard that Indigo spent some time in Reading Jail, hard labor, no one knows why. But you don't find yourself locked up there for stealing crumpets."

"See," Alfie blurted. "It was the Joneses!"

Rohan clapped a hand over his mouth.

"What do you think happened to the Zalindas?" Floppy Hat asked.

"I don't rightly know. Maybe Indigo was so filled with ambition that he sabotaged the rope. He seems capable." Big Collar puffed his chest for his recitation. "'Let me have men about me that are fat . . .' Yond Indigo 'has a lean and hungry look; he thinks too much: such men are dangerous.'"

"You think so?" asked Floppy Hat.

"Oh, I don't know. There is also Karlov, consumed by

jealousy and mad as a hatter. I'll bet he knows more than one way to cut a rope."

"No. He hated Cesar Zalinda, but not the others."

"What you say is rational, but Karlov is not. There is no method in his madness. He's a 'green-ey'd monster which doth mock the meat it feeds on.'"

"I am sorry about the Zalindas, but in the end they were actin' a tad strange, wouldn't you say?" said Floppy Hat. "Keepin' to themselves and refusin' to socialize with the rest of us. And oddest of all, when Cesar disappeared, they didn't talk about it with anyone. Like they wasn't upset or surprised."

"'Tis true. They were also spending time with that rope salesman — what a peculiar sort he was! Another dark one, I tell you. Strangers are always a bad sign, and that one, though dressed like a gentleman, had the air of a rogue. A few days back, I saw the Zalindas returning with him late at night. What could they have been doing?"

Floppy Hat shrugged.

Big Collar motioned to the tightrope. "Now look at all the Joneses up there, like the Zalindas were never here. I guess bad events can bring good things for some people."

"Speakin' of good things," said Floppy Hat, "why don't we go visit Angelina and Balina. I'll entertain Angelina and you can spend time with Balina."

Big Collar smirked. "That Balina is a tough one, but I could be persuaded."

Floppy Hat brushed crumbs from his lap. "I must reapply my cheeks. Then let's pick some wildflowers."

"Ah, yes, to woo their maiden heads." Big Collar chuckled as the two clowns strode off.

"We can stop now. I have had enough." Pilar's voice had an odd pitch.

"We will stop when I say so and not before! You are still much too calm, like the other one." Karlov did a crooked waltz back to his bottle and his knives.

When he threw the fifth knife, which struck the disk by her right ear, Pilar did not make a sound. She simply spun in a blur.

"This is much too easy," Karlov said, lifting a handheld mirror from the table. He turned his back to the disk and picked up another knife. Then, looking into the mirror, which he held in his left hand, he threw the knife over his right shoulder. This time it grazed Pilar's hair as it hit the disk. She screamed.

Ozzie and Wiggins appeared from behind a trunk, carrying a loop of rope. They tossed the loop over Karlov and pulled, pinning his arms to his sides. The burly man struggled and began to curse.

"Let us see how far we can go, shall we?" Wiggins mocked, tying off one end of the rope around Karlov while Ozzie ran with the other end and fed it into the gears behind the spinning disk.

The disk reeled in the rope like fishing line, yanking Karlov from his feet and dragging him across the floor. The weight of him caused the disk to slow.

Karlov came to rest hanging upside down against the gears of the now stationary disk. He barked, "Untie me, you mongrels!"

The boys raced to free Pilar. Together they unbuckled her and helped her down off the disk. She took a second to catch her breath and regain her balance on solid ground, then stumbled dizzily between the boys, who held her beneath the shoulders.

"Let's Scapa Flow!" Wiggins said, realizing that Karlov's shouts could lure in passersby.

"No, wait." Ozzie turned back.

Karlov was struggling against the tightly bound rope, his face a dark red. "Demons, s'blood, get you," he spewed incoherently, and then spit.

"We will cut you down if you tell us what you know about the Zalindas," Ozzie told him.

"To Hades with you all!"

Ozzie pulled one of the knives from the disk and pointed it at Karlov.

Wiggins and Pilar watched nervously.

"You have been drinking, and if you continue to hang upside down, you will pass out. It could be hours before anyone finds you. And if you hang upside down for too long, I think it causes damage to the brain. But suit yourself." Ozzie turned to Wiggins and Pilar. "Come on."

Karlov groaned and stopped swearing. "Wait!" he yelled. "Why do you care what happened to those scoundrels?"

"All we want to know is what you know," Ozzie said.

"Cut me down and I will —"

"Not until you tell us."

"Blast it. Why should I care about those men? They took away my little Penny." Karlov began to sob.

Ozzie kept silent and waited.

"I know nothing about the deaths of those beasts, but I have no doubt it was not an accident. I saw them that night. The four of them went off with my Penny and that rogue who had been spending time with them. They all left in the same carriage.

"I couldn't believe she'd gone after four years of being together. Four years! I was so stunned that I did nothing. Blast it, I did nothing! Hours later they returned, but just the three without the young one or my Penny." Karlov was bawling by now, and his cries pierced the air. "I confronted them, but the three wouldn't speak, and the stranger rode off. Oh, my Penny, why did you leave me?"

Ozzie nodded.

Wiggins told Karlov to prepare to catch himself, and then he cut the rope.

CHAPTER ELEVEN
Ozzie confronts Indigo Jones

Rohan and the boys met up with Ozzie, Wiggins, and Pilar outside Madam Estrella's tent. After they exchanged the information they'd obtained from Karlov and the clowns, all agreed to eliminate Karlov as a suspect. But Big Collar had made some serious accusations about Indigo Jones. So Ozzie suggested they approach him. Since he led the Joneses and had a criminal background, he was the most suspicious. The boys decided that Ozzie should talk to him. After all, he was the best questioner, and Indigo seemed like a tough customer. They all set off for the main tent, but no one anticipated that Indigo might still be up on the tightrope.

"Excuse me, sir, may I speak with you?"

Indigo Jones looked down from his perch at a skinny boy in a bowler hat. It was an odd hour for visitors, he noted. The circus wasn't even open. Indigo scanned the floor for other strays. But he and the boy appeared to be the only ones in the tent.

"I've no time for autographs, can't you see that?" Indigo lifted the balance pole and poised himself to step onto the rope.

"With all due respect, sir, it's not an autograph I've come for."

"No? Then what's your business?" Indigo stood upright, looking straight ahead. From below, his black tights, red handkerchief tied around his bald head, and pointy black triangle beard made him look like an evil joker in a deck of cards.

"More like an interview, about your expertise on the tightrope. My father's a newspaperman with the *Dispatch*. I'm his assistant. We'd like to write an article about you and your act."

Indigo couldn't help but feel flattered. He and his clan hadn't even walked the rope yet, and already their reputation was spreading.

Ozzie pulled a small tablet of paper and a pencil from his coat pocket and waved them in the air like a stick of meat held out to a dog.

Surprisingly, Indigo didn't bite. "As you see, I am busy. If you want to speak with me, come up here." Indigo laughed derisively and stepped onto the rope.

Meanwhile, Pilar and the Irregulars watched from their hiding spot beneath the stands as Indigo trod confidently toward the center pole of the tent.

Ozzie paused, then walked to the base of the center pole and looked up. Suddenly Indigo appeared to be a thousand feet up in the air. Ozzie felt dizzy just watching him. But Master was depending on them, he reminded himself.

Ozzie examined the pegs on either side of the pole. He drew a deep breath, reached out, and began to climb.

"He's gone mad," Rohan whispered to the others.

Pilar didn't say anything, but her left eye twitched, betraying her concern.

"Oz shouldn't leave the ground," Wiggins worried aloud.

Keep talking and stay focused, Ozzie told himself as he grabbed peg after peg. "Mr. Jones, is it difficult to walk the rope after what happened last night?"

Indigo continued walking, his gaze fixed straight ahead.

"I thought this interview was about me and the Joneses — the Royal Family of the Air."

Ozzie climbed steadily and chose his words carefully. "Right. It's just, well, you are clearly brave. Some people would be superstitious about performing so soon."

"Boy, are you trying to make me uncomfortable?" By now Indigo had walked about half the length of the rope.

"Oh no, sir, really I was just wondering if you, as a tight-rope specialist yourself, have any idea what happened to the Zalindas. Since they were your colleagues, you must be quite torn up about their unfortunate demise."

Indigo cleared his throat. "Do you really think this is the time to talk about such things? Better I should tell you how the Joneses will conquer the show circuit with their *amazing* showmanship!"

Ozzie couldn't help but notice Indigo's emphasis on the word *amazing*. Would he take the Zalindas' title, in addition to their act? Had he taken their lives?

Ozzie had been concentrating so profoundly on grasping peg after peg that before he realized it, he was just ten hands below the rope, approximately fifty feet in the air. He looked down at the distant sawdust and felt the contents of his stomach crawl toward his mouth. In a half panic, he stopped and hugged the pole.

"Crud," Wiggins said under his breath. "Fear's set in. That and the effort of climbin' will surely cause trouble for 'im."

"Hold on, Oz," Alfie whispered, and soon all the boys and Pilar were quietly cheering him on.

Ozzie's arms and legs were twisted around the pole like noodles around a fork, and his feet rested weakly on the pegs. He should not have stopped, he realized too late. He should never have looked down. His vision blurred, and he began to wheeze.

"You look a bit green there, boy. How do you feel being up here after what happened last night?" Indigo chuckled darkly. "I should like to help you, but as you see, I have my hands full." He indicated the balance pole by raising it arrogantly above his head like a weight lifter, then returned it to its original position by his waist.

Ozzie closed his eyes, swallowed the metallic taste in his mouth, and asked, "Did you ever meet the rope salesman?"

Still amused, Indigo said, "Boy, you have enough troubles now, without worrying about the likes of Orlando Vile."

Pegs, hands, pegs, hands, Ozzie chanted inside like a mantra. It

"Mr. Jones, I believe you know something about the deaths of the Zalindas."

was so simple. If he could just pretend he were a mere two feet from the ground, he could manage the remainder of the climb easily. Determined, Ozzie unwrapped himself from the pole and reached for the next peg. Meanwhile, he stored the name Orlando Vile in his memory.

"Do you think there was a problem with the rope, or was it something else?" Ozzie asked, regaining his composure.

"Why are you asking such questions? Who are you?" Indigo walked less formally now, moving with an uneasy gait. He had traveled three-quarters of the way across the rope, and Ozzie could see that his face was red.

At last Ozzie reached the perch, a round board, four feet in diameter attached to the tent pole. He drew a deep breath and looked directly at Indigo, now just a few feet away. "Mr. Jones, I believe you know something about the deaths of the Zalindas. You do not have to speak to me, but you may find it less bothersome than speaking to the authorities."

Indigo strode angrily toward Ozzie.

Ozzie couldn't help but recoil.

"What do we do?" Pilar asked Wiggins.

"Just wait," he answered.

When Indigo reached the perch, instead of clutching Ozzie around the neck as Ozzie had anticipated, he calmly placed the balance pole in the rack above them. He curled one foot at a time, cracking his toes, then repeated the gesture with his fingers. He peered menacingly into Ozzie's eyes. "Tell me who you work for before I toss you on your arse." He pointed to the floor of the tent. "There is no One here to witness it."

Ozzie could feel his heart beating unevenly, and he feared a sudden attack of asthma. "Another death here would be bad for business," he managed.

Indigo grabbed the front of Ozzie's coat, knocking off his bowler, which spun saucerlike as it fell toward the ground.

Suddenly there was a commotion down below.

"You makin' friends up there, Oz!" Wiggins yelled, racing out from beneath the stands to the center of the ring.

The rest of the boys and Pilar followed, all making a general ruckus.

"You always said you wanted to run away to the circus!"

"You finally get your audition?"

Indigo looked down. "What is all this?!" he demanded.

"As far as I can see, it's quite a lot of witnesses," Ozzie told Indigo plainly. "Now, if you would kindly let go of me, sir."

Indigo opened his grasp.

"The Zalindas were murdered, Mr. Jones, and we can prove it. If you are not involved, you have no reason to withhold information. Keeping silent might suggest you are guilty."

Indigo began to shake, not with anger but something else. Was it fear? Ozzie wondered.

"I know nothing. And even if I did, I see no point in sharing it with the likes of you." Indigo turned, reclaimed the balance pole, and stepped back onto the rope. "I am warning you, boy," he said gravely. "You are in over your head, and you know not the danger you are delving into. Trust me when I say that if you probe too far, you will not live to tell your tale."

CHAPTER TWELVE
Pilar reveals her powers

After Ozzie recovered from his encounter with Indigo, he, Wiggins, Pilar, and the boys walked back to Madam Estrella's tent. Since PilaR's mother wasn't there, they had a private spot to exchange ideas about the murder. And the dry tent was a refuge from the damp air outside. Plus, Madam Estrella always kept a jar of gingerbread, which Pilar passed around, so the boys feasted happily as they talked.

"Well, it seems we've done as much as we can," Ozzie said after a few minutes. "I think it's time we report back to Master. He'll be eager to hear that we've got a name for the rope salesman."

Wiggins nodded in agreement.

As the boys stood to go, Pilar stood, too. "Wait!" she said anxiously. "I mean, it's just . . . well . . . we haven't really learned anything yet. You should stay. We'll go find Barboza and question him." Could they hear the disappointment in her voice? she wondered. Did they know she was weary of circus life and hungry for friends her own age?

Ozzie considered her kindly. "It's not a bad idea, but Master has already spoken to Barboza. There's nothing more he'll share with us."

"The rest of the Joneses, then. Maybe one of them will reveal more information," Pilar suggested.

Wiggins shook his head. "After Ozzie's meeting with Indigo, surely he told the others not to talk to us."

Unanimously, the boys agreed that they had done what they could and should return to Baker Street.

Pilar tried to hide her upset. Coolly, she sat down in front of her mother's crystal ball. "Before you go, then, I would like to give you a reading, all of you. I might see some things that can help."

Ozzie and Wiggins looked at each other.

Wiggins shrugged. He was curious about the crystal ball that sat on the table like a beautiful, giant marble.

"You didn't say you could tell fortunes," Ozzie remarked.

"Isn't it plain? I am a Gypsy and the daughter of a fortune-teller. The powers are in my blood. Now, please, turn down the lanterns."

"Okay, but you must do it quickly. Master is waiting for us." Ozzie sat down on the same stool he'd sat on earlier, noting he had gone his whole life without a single reading and here he was having two in one day.

Rohan dimmed the lanterns, then joined the rest of the boys, who had gathered in a semicircle on stools surrounding Pilar.

Pilar closed her eyes and stroked the crystal. In the darkness of the tent, the ball began to glow. Pilar chanted softly in another language, maybe Spanish or Romani; the boys could not tell. When she opened her eyes, only the whites showed, which caused a few of the boys to gasp.

"The man you seek dies more than once. Like water, you can hold him, but he will pour through your fingers." The voice that came from Pilar was of a much older woman, and it boomed. "You are nothing to him, pocket lint to be discarded."

Wiggins's eyes went wide with disbelief.

Ozzie watched Pilar carefully.

"You are facing dark times...."

"You are facing dark times," she continued. "Your safety is not guaranteed. Remain as a group and you may survive. Act alone and you will surely die."

Pilar then pointed to Ozzie. "The man you are so desperate to find is not who you believe him to be." Her voice began to change, melting to softness, tenderness.

Ozzie felt an uncomfortable prickling run down his spine. The voice was haunting and familiar. Where had he heard it before?

Pilar continued, "Live your life, son, as if the present is all."

His mother's voice! But it sounded different, tortured, and it was coming from this Gypsy girl's mouth. Was this a trick? And if the spirit of his mother were speaking through Pilar, what was she trying to tell him? That she did not want him to find his father? Why?

Ozzie slid off his stool and began crawling backward away from the others.

As he crept, crablike, toward the door of the tent, the voice continued, "You have more than one father. One will lead you; the other will hurt you. Forget them both. . . ." Pilar began to groan and growl, like a sick animal. Foam came flowing from her mouth, and then, with a startling thud, she fell forward onto the table, her body popping with convulsions.

In that moment, the crystal ball rolled off its base, across the table, and onto the floor. The boys screamed, and Ozzie reached the tent door just in time to back up hard against someone entering.

"Pilar! *¡Dímelo ahora mismo, hija!* Tell me right now what's going on here, daughter!"

Wiggins rushed over to turn up the lanterns.

Pilar lifted her head languidly. "Nothing, Mamá," she said in her own voice, though she appeared dazed and her speech was slow. "The boys asked me for a reading, so I went along. It was harmless."

Madam Estrella's eyes were fierce. "*Hija,* you know not the strength of your powers. Using your gift for fun is irresponsible and dangerous."

Pilar looked at her hands, which trembled like butterfly wings. She bent down to pick up the crystal ball and placed it carefully back on its base. "Yes, Mamá."

"I am warning you, boys," Madam Estrella told the group. "You would be wise to disregard everything this girl has said. She has a strong tendency toward exaggeration, don't you, *hija?*"

"If you say so, Mamá," Pilar answered, slowly regaining her composure.

"Now, if you would leave us to ourselves," Madam Estrella said, looking from Pilar back to the boys. "My daughter and I have some things to discuss."

The boys rushed out of the tent. But as Wiggins strode past Pilar, she whispered, "It was all true. I wouldn't lie to you."

Moments later, in the cart headed toward Baker Street, Rohan said, "I never seen nothin' like that. Was it an act, Ozzie?"

Ozzie lifted his chin from his bent knees. "I only believe what I can see and what can be explained logically. There's no explanation for what happened to Pilar. And yet, I don't think it was an act, despite Madam Estrella's warning."

"Yeah, I believed her when she said she wouldn't lie to us," Wiggins added, "even though we hardly know her. It's just a feeling I've got in me bones."

Ozzie nodded, then rested his chin back on his knees. "The question is, what does it mean for us?"

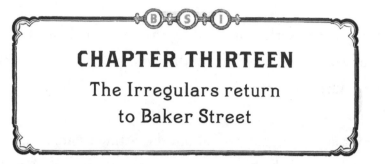

CHAPTER THIRTEEN
The Irregulars return
to Baker Street

When the boys arrived at Baker Street, Billy, the page, met them at the door of 221 B. His eyes were large with news. "Master just received a correspondence he'd been expectin' from Switzerland." Billy put a finger to his lips, warning the boys to keep quiet about it, then went up to announce their presence.

Ozzie and Wiggins entered the sitting room. Watson lowered his paper and nodded to them, while Holmes flipped noisily through his correspondence and paced the room. He did not look up or say anything.

As Ozzie stood waiting to speak with Holmes, he could feel his pulse race. Here he was inside Master's flat, face-to-face with him! He tried to calm himself by studying the man. He was quite tall and lean, with an aquiline nose. His eyes were sharp, and his hands appeared surprisingly strong for a gentleman. Reading the letter, he looked like an actor standing before his audience. And he moved gracefully, like a dancer or maybe a boxer. Definitely a boxer, Ozzie decided.

Ozzie let his gaze drift about the sitting room. A fireplace mantel framed the lower portion of the north wall. A rack of pipes sat upon the mantel, and beneath it hung a Persian slipper. Tobacco tins and cigar boxes were stacked in the coal scuttle to the left of the fireplace, and all manner of laboratory equipment was lined up on a table along the east wall. The south wall was dotted with bullet holes that formed the letters *V* and *R*, each approximately fifteen inches high. A violin rested on a stack of books in the corner.

A violin! Ozzie couldn't help but recall Madam Estrella's reading. She'd seen a man watching over him and heard violin musIc. What else had Madam Estrella said? Ozzie was trying hard to recall when Wiggins elbowed him in the side. He looked up to see Holmes, Watson, and Wiggins all staring at him.

"Is there something wrong with his hearing?" asked Watson.

"No, sir," Wiggins responded, looking at Ozzie quizzically.

Holmes stepped up and examined Ozzie head to toe. "Wiggins, how long has he been with the gang?" he asked, still staring at Ozzie.

"Two or three months, sir."

"What is your name, lad?"

"Osgood Manning."

"And you are, let me guess, twelve years old."

"In a few weeks' time, sir."

"Hmm . . . and not from London. Oxfordshire, most likely."

"Yes, sir, Banbury."

Holmes studied Ozzie thoughtfully. "Does your boss, the scrivener, know that you wander the streets with the rest of the Irregulars?"

A deduction, Ozzie realized, emerging more fully from his reverie. Master had looked at him and, like magic, was able to tell who he was. Think, *think*, he pushed himself.

Holmes opened his mouth to speak, but before he could, Ozzie blurted, "I find deductions very exciting, sir. If I may . . ."

Holmes nodded his consent, amusement playing at the corners of his mouth.

"Don't forget, boys," Holmes continued, *"mediocrity knows nothing higher than itself, but talent always recognizes genius."*

"My accent gave away where I grew up, and my hand, specifically the middle finger on my right hand," Ozzie said, offering up his calloused finger for closer examination, "reveals that I write quite a lot. Since I can write, I can obviously read. I speak more properly than my station would suggest. But from my dress and my association with the Irregulars, it is clear I am not affluent. Thus, in what situation could a young literate person of humble means find himself? A scrivener's apprentice. If you please, sir, am I correct?"

Watson's jaw dropped.

Wiggins clapped a hand over his mouth to hide his smile.

Holmes tilted his head to the side, watching Ozzie like a hawk contemplating a promising fledgling. "I see, Wiggins, why you chose to bring your new friend along. In our last few cases together, I have sensed an organizing presence amongst your ranks, someone with special abilities. Pray, Osgood, where did you receive your education?"

"I have little formal training, sir, but was taught by my grandfather, a retired schoolmaster. Thank you for the compliment. It's an honor working for you."

"Don't forget, boys," Holmes continued, "mediocrity

knows nothing higher than itself, but talent always recognizes genius. You, my young friends, have talent. Now if you will, please share what you learned at the circus."

Wiggins began to tell their tale and deferred to Ozzie at the appropriate times for information he had learned directly.

When Ozzie shared that Karlov saw Cesar and Penelope leave with the rest of the Zalindas and never return, Holmes nodded. Then Wiggins described in detail, with dramatic flourishes, Ozzie's questioning of Indigo Jones on the tightrope. "And just when Jones had Ozzie 'round the throat, the lot of us rushed —"

"We are not daredevils, boys," Holmes interrupted. "There may be times when I am called upon to face danger, but I do not expect that from you." He turned toward Ozzie. "Approaching Jones in that manner was reckless."

Ozzie and Wiggins looked down at their feet, their excitement suddenly diminished from the scolding.

Holmes paced the room and lifted his pipe from the desk. He waved at the boys to continue.

"I did learn the name of the rope salesman," Ozzie offered.

Holmes was lighting his pipe, but stopped with the match held midair.

Watson laughed. "My goodness, Holmes. You were trying a good part of the morning to discover that."

Holmes smiled lightly, extinguished the flame, and gestured with his pipe. "Pray, young man, kindly share the name that has escaped me these past several hours."

"Orlando Vile."

"Vile!" Holmes yelled, and then in a restrained fashion asked, "Are you sure, Osgood?"

"Yes, sir."

Holmes clapped his hands loudly and, without saying another word, paced across the room to his index and opened it excitedly. He then picked up his commonplace book of biographies.

"Let's see, Section V, just before our friend Villard. Vile, Orlando." Holmes traced his forefinger down the page and paraphrased. "Formerly first mate on the HMS *Martin*; leads an unsuccessful mutiny in the waters off Tristan da Cunha in '82; kills two officers before he is stopped; arrested, but on the return to Portsmouth for court-martial proceedings escapes from custody off the coast of Africa. Surfaces sometime later as a merchant in Fez. Flees Morocco after a series of grand thefts. Returns to London five years ago with some financial standing; functions under different aliases. Master planner of thefts. The fourth most dangerous man in London."

Holmes set aside the volume, lifted his pipe to his mouth, and puffed it.

"Sir, if you don't mind me askin', why would a man like that have business with the Zalindas?" said Wiggins.

Wiggins's question reminded Ozzie of one that had been gnawing at him. "And why are you looking into the deaths of the Zalindas when you have been engaged by the Prince of Wales?" he added.

Holmes smiled. "Aha. You boys appear to know of my most illustrious client. Let me say preliminarily that the events at the circus and the palace are related and the link between them, I believe, is this man Vile."

Holmes stood and strode to his desk. He scribbled a quick note, then rang the bell for Billy. When he appeared, Holmes said, "Billy, please take this to the telegraph office. They will know where to send it."

Billy nodded, took the note and some change, and exited.

"Now then," Holmes said, returning his attention to Ozzie and Wiggins, "before I explain the grand theft committed at the palace, I shall provide a short history lesson. Please have a seat." Holmes pointed to a coach settee. "For you to understand anything about the case of the Zalindas, you must first learn of *The Stuart Chronicle.*"

CHAPTER FOURTEEN
Holmes shares the tale of
The Stuart Chronicle

The boys settled into the velvet settee with cups of hot tea that Mrs. Hudson delivered on a silver tray. Wiggins thought he had never felt so posh. But what was one to do with a cup *and* saucer? He stole glances at Ozzie, who cradled the saucer in the palm of his left hand and circled the thumb and forefinger of his right around the loop of the delicate teacup. He sipped slowly, replacing the cup on the saucer after each swallow. Wiggins did the same, though somewhat more noisily. It was difficult to keep the saucer balanced in his bandaged hand. As they drank, the boys waited for Holmes to begin his tale.

"You lads may not be aware of a disruption of the monarchy in the mid-1600s, when a man named Cromwell beheaded our king, Charles I. Charles I was a member of the House of

Stuart. The eleven-year period that followed his murder is known as the Commonwealth and the Protectorate. During this time, members of the royal family went into hiding. In one of my earliest cases, the Musgrave Ritual, I had the pleasure of unearthing treasure that had belonged to King Charles I and been hidden for Charles II.

"Once the monarchy was restored, the Stuart family returned to the throne. At this point, King Charles II took various steps to secure his position and celebrate the renewed order in the land. Most of these steps were known to the public, but a few were of the most private nature.

"In one such private gesture, Charles II commissioned the creation of a grand chronicle. The pages of this magnificent book were made of the finest parchment, the edges trimmed in gold. The cover was gilded in solid gold and shimmered with the dust of the rarest gems and stones, held by the royals since the time of the Crusades."

Holmes sat back in an upholstered Armchair, his legs crossed. He stoked his pipe and continued. "Charles II created this chronicle as a private diary to record the thoughts and insights of every monarch. The book was to be passed from generation to generation as a guide for governance. For more than two hundred years, despite wars and disputes within the monarchy, the *Chronicle* acted as a link, giving continuity to the throne.

"Undoubtedly, *The Stuart Chronicle*, as it has since been named, must be one of the most valuable books in the world, both for its secrets and its gems. Few members of the royal family even know of its existence. It is only for the eyes of the king or queen in power.

"Until yesterday, I had only heard speculation of such a book. When I was summoned by Her Majesty Queen Victoria, through her son Prince Edward, I learned that such a chronicle does in fact exist. As you appear to be aware, I was taken to the palace to investigate a theft. And as you now may guess, the *Chronicle* of which I have spoken has been stolen, in one of the most unique thefts of all time."

Wiggins dropped his cup on the saucer with a loud clink. He and Ozzie looked at each other in awe.

"Apparently the *Chronicle* was kept in a small third-floor study, accessible only to Her Majesty and her most personal aides. The door to the room remained locked at all times,

"Undoubtedly, The Stuart Chronicle, *as it has since been named, must be one of the most valuable books in the world, both for its secrets and its gems."*

though the window was less than secure. The *Chronicle* had last been seen a few days prior.

"Wiggins, you have witnessed my methods. When I arrived at the palace, I observed the ground in the area below the room in question and observed the wall of the palace itself. I saw no irregularities.

"The prince proceeded to lead me into the palace and up to the study, which involved walking through a catacomb of rooms on the third floor. The area was quite secure, with a guard assigned to stand permanent watch at the door of the study.

"The room itself was small but quite lavish, with oak shelves lining the walls, a large carpet of Persian design on the floor, a silk-covered settee in the corner, and a grand desk with a side table where the *Chronicle* was last seen. Above the desk were two windows.

"I examined the carpet and the desk and found no disturbance. Proceeding to the window, I examined the casing and the glass. Again I found not a single mark. I then opened the window and saw at last a clue — an oval smudge, a footlike mark. But it was not a bare footprint or the tracing of a shoe sole. It was the smudge of a slipper."

Ozzie's brow wrinkled. A slipper, a slipper, he thought, and a picture began to form in his mind. Indigo Jones had been wearing slippers when Ozzie confronted him. Ozzie became excited. He suddenly knew where all of this was going — the circus, the palace, it was all the same. "Tightrope walkers wear slippers," he said, the words exiting his mouth before he realized he'd spoken them aloud.

Holmes raised an eyebrow. "You have a quick mind indeed, Osgood. From there, things moved quite swiftly. Out the window, I observed the fence that surrounded the grounds. I proceeded down to the second-floor area directly below the study and saw that it was a little-used music room. In my examination of the window frames, there were not only the slipper prints — the size of a man's foot — but pressure marks on the window frame, suggesting a board and some bars had been pushed against it with great force. Most important, on the sill of the frame, there were scratches as well as fibers consistent with a rope. Looking across the way, I saw that the top of the fence that protected the palace appeared some ten feet lower than the window.

"From this, I deduced that a thief had scaled the fence and run across the courtyard dragging a rope behind him.

An accomplice within the palace lowered a line out the second-floor window, which the thief managed to climb up, still dragging the rope behind him. Through some mechanism, the rope was then pulled with great force until it was completely taut, running from the top of the fence to the second-floor window. At that point, our thief was joined by his accomplices, who walked across the inclined rope to the side of the building. Standing on the rope and steadied against the wall, the thieves made a human tower. The last of them scaled up his cohorts, entered the study window easily, and took the *Chronicle*. Then, retracing the steps in reverse, they escaped, leaving nary a clue."

"The Joneses?" Wiggins said, attempting his own deduction.

Ozzie nudged him softly in the ribs and shook his head.

Master was too absorbed in his recitation to hear the mistake.

"My investigation continued at the bars of the fence, which I believed the thieves had scaled. To my surprise, I saw a large spot of dried blood on the other side. I have my suspicions as to how it was formed, but that is for another time.

"Upon leaving the palace, I made various inquiries, for I suspected some acrobats were involved in this crime. You can imagine how surprised I was to read about the deaths of the Zalindas this morning. I was sure that they were the culprits. Now learning that Vile is involved only confirms what I already suspected."

Understanding registered on Wiggins's face. "But who killed the Zalindas?" he asked.

"Vile planned the theft and engaged the Zalindas. After they obtained the *Chronicle*, they were of no use and, further, posed a threat, for they knew who had the *Chronicle*."

"Pray, Holmes, what happened to the fourth Zalinda then, Cesar?" Watson asked.

"He's dead," said Ozzie. "That was his blood, wasn't it?" He looked at Holmes.

"Yes, my boy, I believe it was. Somehow that young acrobat fell from the rope. Very strange indeed."

"What about Penelope?" Ozzie asked.

"We shall see, for we're not done here," Holmes said, scraping out his pipe and reaching for another plug of tobacco. "Indeed, boys, we have only just begun our investigation."

CHAPTER FIFTEEN
Ozzie at the
scrivener's shop

O zzie and Wiggins parted outside Holmes's flat. In spite of Ozzie's excitement about finally meeting Master, the good feelings of the day diminished with every stride as he made his way back to the scrivener's shop. It was late afternoon, and the sky had thickened into a gruel gray. Ozzie had never dared to be away from the shop for so long, and the fear of Crumbly's reaction weighed on him.

But today was special, he reminded himself, with the intrigue of a new case involving the circus, the prince, the palace, and *The Stuart Chronicle*. Best of all, he had even impressed Holmes with his deduction. Ozzie jingled the coins he had earned, including the guinea for discovering Vile's name. He pulled the money from his pocket and counted it, then returned it. He pictured his biscuit tin filling with

Sometimes Ozzie wished he'd never discovered his copying skills. Then maybe Crumbly would have thought him useless and tossed him out onto the street.

change that would help him search out his father. And yet, as he approached the shop, not even that thought or the music of the silver could drown out his anxiety.

Sometimes Ozzie wished he'd never discovered his copying skills. Then maybe Crumbly would have thought him useless and tossed him out onto the street.

He remembered that fateful afternoon when he'd been sweeping the room where the scriveners sat. Alone and bored, but happy to read anything, Ozzie glanced over at one of the desks and saw two matching documents side by side. It wasn't just that Frankie, the principal scrivener, had copied a document, he had made an *identical* copy, right down to the signatures that appeared at the bottom of the pages. Ozzie was mesmerized.

Frankie returned from an errand in time to catch Ozzie examining his work. "What are you doing, lad? Can you even read?"

Ozzie froze, not knowing what to say. "Yes," he answered as he went back to sweeping.

Frankie seemed a decent sort, and though Crumbly had a few others who worked for him regularly, only Frankie was in the shop every day. He took a blank sheet of paper off a ream. "Come over here and give it a try."

Hesitantly, Ozzie climbed up on a stool. Frankie handed him a quill. "Try the first line. Look at the writing and then picture what the writer was feeling, not by the words, but by the shape and form of the letters. Study the lines and the angles, then think about who wrote it. I can see the man who wrote this note — it's so clear I'd know him on the street."

Ozzie examined the first line of text. The letters were made with narrow loops, and they were evenly spaced but tightly packed. The letters were thin and neat, and they leaned forward, like they were running across the line.

Ozzie started to write slowly and, when he felt a bit more confident, he scribbled down the rest of the line. He paused and looked at it.

Frankie took the page and held it up to the original. He grinned. "Try the next line," he said, putting the sheet before Ozzie.

Ozzie looked at the writing again. This was written by a particular sort, he recognized, a perfectionist, who was tense and in a hurry. Ozzie closed his eyes and tried to picture the man. When he opened his eyes, he wrote the line straight through.

Frankie picked up the sheet and compared it to the original. "Mate, you have talent."

From then on, Ozzie watched the goings-on in the shop more carefully. Now and again, shopkeepers and tradesmen would enter the front door with small jobs — shop records or contracts — to be copied. But the biggest jobs almost always came in through the back door, brought by rough-looking men who were curiously well dressed. They often insisted on waiting in the shop until the copying work was completed, even if it took all day. Only the most experienced scriveners, like Frankie, were assigned such work.

Ozzie soon realized that Crumbly and his crew were master forgers. Wills, promissory notes, bank records, bills of sale, whatever needed to be recreated, Oxford Scriveners could do the job. Though they took on some legitimate copy work through the front door, most of what they duplicated came in through the back.

As the weeks passed, Frankie began to give Ozzie tips on forgery, and Ozzie's skills flourished. Frankie alerted Crumbly to Ozzie's extraordinary talent, and he was soon put to work on small jobs.

"I guess I have meself a Real apprentice," Crumbly said with great satisfaction.

Eventually, he let the part-timers go because Ozzie forged better than all of them, and he didn't cost a cent.

Ozzie enjoyed picturing the writers of the documents he forged. He felt he could tell what they were like and how they were feeling just by reading their handwriting. But after he mastered the skill, forging documents became a bore. There was little mind-work involved.

Now, dreading even the inky smell of the shop, Ozzie opened the front door. He passed through the small antechamber into the workshop area. To his relief, all was quiet. Frankie had left, which was a good sign — business was slow and Crumbly was likely at the pub or passed out in his flat above the shop.

But as Ozzie crept back toward the storage room where he slept, a metal cup bounced off the wall over his head. He spun around in time to see a metal plate flying toward him. He ducked and crouched behind a writing table as the plate crashed into the wall.

"You vermin, makin' a fool of me!" Crumbly barreled out of his office, spit flying from his lips. He picked up a large book and threw it, knocking an inkwell off the table, just missing Ozzie.

"Where you been, you little beggar? I've been soft with ye, I have, and now you've made a laughin'stock of me, runnin' off all day." Crumbly had a head of flaming red hair and large pork chop–size sideburns to match. Though quite short, he was thick and powerfully built. Grog sores covered his nose and face. His plaid woolen vest fit tightly around his belly, buttons popping. His cuffs were rolled up, his collar wrinkled. He bumped into a table as he flew across the room.

Ozzie circled around the shop, trying to keep his distance.

But running away only inflamed Crumbly more. "C'm'ere, you maggot!" Crumbly scurried on his thick, stumpy legs and tried to corner Ozzie.

"We have the biggest job of me whole bleedin' career comin' in tomorrow. Jack Crumbly is finally havin' his due. Them chains are in the back, and you'll be wearin' 'em tonight!"

Ozzie panicked. Being chained up sounded horrible, but tonight it would be an absolute disaster, for he and Wiggins had arranged to meet Master later.

Ozzie moved to dodge Crumbly, but the angry little man hit him square in the stomach with his fist. The air shot out of Ozzie's lungs as he doubled over.

Crumbly locked his sausagelike arm around Ozzie's neck and dragged him across the shop toward the back storage room.

"We are about to rise to a whole 'nother class, and I won't 'ave you muckin' it up. The master of 'em all has tapped me!" With this, he gave Ozzie's neck a yank for emphasis.

"Tomorrow's job will make Jack Crumbly famous in the right circles. Big pay, handsome pay!" Crumbly laughed and spit.

As they entered the storage room, Ozzie caught a glimpse of the wrist irons that had been bolted to the wall over his pallet.

"From now on, I'll be chainin' you up at night. No more wanderin' off."

He threw Ozzie down on the pallet and grabbed and twisted his arm as he reached for a chain.

"Wait, sir," Ozzie squeaked, grunting with pain. "If you chain my wrists, I may not be able to write tomorrow. My hands will be numb." He waited for his words to register on Crumbly's face, then added with false conviction, "But I am sure that Frankie can do the job."

Crumbly stopped and looked at the chain and then at Ozzie. They both knew that Ozzie's talent at forgery was matched only by his speed. Plus, he worked for free. Pausing, Crumbly howled and dropped Ozzie's arm. "I knew I should 'ave had 'em put in the ankle irons!" he shouted, and kicked the pallet. "All right then, but yer not goin' nowhere." Crumbly pushed Ozzie onto the pallet and marched out of the storage room, locking the door behind him.

When he was sure that Crumbly had left the shop, Ozzie reached under the pallet and pulled out a small oil lamp. He arranged the taper and struck a match to light it. He removed a loose brick from the wall and slid out a small tin biscuit box. In it were the coins he'd been saving up and a few keepsakes. Ozzie added his pay from Holmes to the box. He then lifted a small tintype of his mother. In the thin metal-plated photograph, she wore her good dress and had a reserved but pleasant smile. It had been taken about three years back, before she grew ill, when they still lived with Grandfather in the countryside.

If his mother had known the nature of Crumbly's business, she never would have left him here. If only he could live with the gang in the carriage factory, he'd be so much better off. But Ozzie knew that if he ran away now, Crumbly would surely inform the authorities or hire some roughs to find him.

He looked up at the window, which abutted the ceiling in the corner of the storage room. The sad, gray light of early evening leaked in.

Ozzie had studied the window on prior occasions when he'd been locked up. It was small and square, and even on a bright day let in little light. Ozzie considered a pile of crates across from him and then looked back up at the window. He knew it was a steep drop to the street below, but he didn't care. His head should fit through, and the rest would follow, he thought, redepositing the picture of his mother in the biscuit tin and hiding it back in the wall. An injury, a beating, even the threat of the police — none of that mattered now. Wiggins and Holmes were waiting for him.

CHAPTER SIXTEEN
Elliot performs surgery

Back at the Castle, the boys were finishing a meal of beans and sausage on rolls. Wiggins always held a certain percentage of the wages from Holmes for rations and stretched it out for periods when they were not in Master's employ. But tonight they feasted.

Ozzie slipped carefully through the trapdoor, holding his side, his right elbow akimbo. He limped over to the fire ring and collapsed on the floor with a groan.

"You all right, mate? You're walkin' like an old man." Wiggins tore off a piece of his sausage and bean roll and held it out to Ozzie.

Ozzie waved it off. He sighed and pulled off his coat. The right side of his shirt was red with blood.

"Blazes, a flash flood! What happened to you?" Wiggins exclaimed.

"You get in a fight, Oz? Who was it? I'll slaughter 'im!" Alfie said, slamming his fist into his palm.

Ozzie shook his head. "Tonight's escape from Crumbly involved a drop from a high window. I landed on a sharp scrap of metal." Carefully, Ozzie slipped off his shirt. A short, deep gash showed itself from beneath the blood.

"Oz, that's a bad one." Wiggins pulled a handkerchief from his pocket and wiped Ozzie's side. "The bleedin's heavy. I don't think you're goin' to meet Master tonight."

"It's not too bad. Master said to be at the docks at ten. We have a few hours yet."

"You'll have to lie still for a while then. We need to fix you up." By now, Ozzie's blood had soaked clear through the handkerchief. "Stitch, get your needle. Rohan, fill a bucket with water from the rain barrel outside. And Alfie, bring that bottle of spirits you found in the back closet."

Elliot got his cigar box, where he kept his sewing supplies. He removed his coat and rolled up his sleeves. He tied a rolled rag around his forehead and dipped one of his larger needles in the bucket of water boiling on the fire. In the rainwater bucket, he washed his hands with a small plug of soap. His movements were businesslike and he spoke to no one.

Wiggins found the cleanest cloth available, a piece of white linen, and tore it in half. He put one piece aside and dunked the other half in the hot water. As Elliot dried his needle, Wiggins cleaned the wound.

Ozzie recoiled from his touch.

Alfie appeared with a small bottle of whiskey. He opened it, took a whiff, and grimaced. "You're not drinkin' this poison are you, Oz?"

Ozzie gave him a weak smile. Seeing Elliot's needle, he felt his stomach lurch.

"We'll see how it goes," Wiggins said. He took the bottle from Alfie and bathed the wound in whiskey. The boys had learned from Watson about keeping wounds, and anything that touched them, clean. Watson loved to tell old war stories from his days in the army of having to perform surgery in the worst conditions.

Ozzie winced.

Wiggins patted his shoulder. "Hang in there, mate. The pain's goin' to get much worse."

With quick, practiced hand movements, Elliot unspooled thick, new thread and slipped it through the needle. One of the boys held up a lantern, and Elliot waved him forward.

"Now come closer with that light. There's surgery here!"

"You ready, Oz?" Wiggins asked.

Ozzie nodded.

"Hold his arms," Elliot instructed Rohan. "You lie across his legs," he said, pointing to Alfie. "And I need you to keep the blood out of my way with that cloth," he told Wiggins. "Now come closer with that light. There's surgery here!"

Elliot pinched Ozzie's skin together at the bottom of the wound and pushed the needle through.

Ozzie bit down hard on his lower lip.

"You need to breathe," Wiggins told him, pouring more whiskey over the wound.

Elliot pushed the needle into Ozzie's skin again, and when it came clear through both sides of the wound, he looped it over and through again in a neat, tracklike pattern. He worked smoothly and delicately and with surprising speed.

"Whiskey, wipe, whiskey, wipe," Elliot dictated to Wiggins as sweat formed on his brow. "Bring the bloody light closer! You don't want me to stitch 'im to his own trousers, do ya?"

Ozzie's jaw clenched, and he tried hard to stifle his groans. His whole body felt alternately hot, then cold. He forced his eyes shut. But the next time the needle pierced his flesh, he screamed and bolted upright.

"Bloody 'eck!" Elliot barked. "Hold 'im down, Wiggins!"

"Steady, mate. Lie back now. We're almost through 'ere."

Ozzie let Wiggins ease him back down, but when the needle bit into his skin again, he howled.

Wiggins mopped his brow. "Elliot's almost done. Just don't look down."

Ozzie kept quiet, but his leg convulsed reflexively, causing him to kick up. Alfie could barely hold on.

"All right. That's it. Easier than makin' a pair of stockings," Elliot joked as he wound up his last stroke with the needle, then cut the thread with a razor.

Wiggins cleaned around the wound with a rinsed cloth and examined the nine stitches. Rohan and Alfie moved back, as Wiggins instructed, to give Ozzie space to breathe.

Elliot took a dry piece of linen, folded it in thirds, and placed it over the stitches. Then he cut a long strip off the bottom of Ozzie's shirt and tied it around his waist to hold the linen in place.

Ozzie moaned and closed his eyes.

"Is he goin' to die?" Alfie asked.

Wiggins looked at Elliot, suddenly nervous. Ozzie's body was frail on his best of days. Maybe it had been foolish of them to stitch him up on their own.

"He ain't goin' to bloody die!" Elliot kept up with the cool cloths on Ozzie's forehead.

"Why ain't he talkin'?" Rohan asked.

"I think he fainted," Wiggins said.

The rest of the gang watched Ozzie's labored breathing and waited quietly.

Minutes ticked by. Five, then ten, but it felt like an eternity to the boys, sitting there in the cold carriage factory on that dark September evening.

Then, into the stillness, Ozzie coughed. "Wiggins?"

"Here I am, mate."

Ozzie opened his eyes and coughed again. "Is the surgery done? We can't be late for Master."

Wiggins motioned to Alfie to go get Ozzie's tonic. "Oz, you're not goin' nowhere tonight. You just got stitched up."

"You only have nine stitches, but if you stretch too much you'll rip out all my work and make a bloody mess," Elliot said matter-of-factly as he returned his supplies to his cigar box. "Now get me some beans," he called to no one in particular. "All that blood-and-guts work makes me hungry."

Wiggins looked at Ozzie. "You heard Stitch — you shouldn't move about tonight."

Ozzie sat up slowly. "I admire Stitch's work, and trust it will hold. I will take some sausage and beans now." He flashed Wiggins a grin.

"Well, you're hungry. That's a good sign. But you're stayin' put tonight," Wiggins said, and went to get him a plate of food. When he returned, Ozzie was standing. Rohan had gotten him another shirt. Gingerly, he slipped it on.

"Master is counting on me," Ozzie told Wiggins. "I promise you, when this is all over, I'll rest."

"Yes, you look like you need it," a voice observed from outside the boys' circle.

The Irregulars spun around and froze as a caped figure materialized inside the Trapdoor.

"Stop!" Wiggins ordered.

But the intruder just strode calmly toward them. "Good evening, boys."

The boys stared at Pilar as if she were a ghost. Other than Billy, no one outside the Irregulars had ever entered the Castle.

"Are you okay?" Pilar asked Ozzie.

He nodded.

"How did you find us?" Wiggins asked.

Pilar nonchalantly surveyed the surroundings. Then she approached the fire purposefully. Several boys in her path faded back. "It was easy. I learned the address of Mr. Holmes from one of the police officers at the circus. I guess everyone has heard of 221 B Baker Street. When Mamá went to sleep, I caught a ride to Mr. Holmes's flat. The boy who met me at the door was quite talkative. Once he knew I was a friend of yours, he was happy to tell me where to find you."

The boys stared at Pilar as if she were a ghost.

"We'll have to educate Billy 'bout what happens to those who speak too freely 'bout us," Wiggins said sternly.

"I thought you might want to know that Indigo Jones has left the circus," Pilar continued. "I spoke with one of his sisters, Irma. She swears he had nothing to do with the Zalindas' deaths, but he was concerned that the police would arrest him because of his criminal record."

"We know who the murderer is," said Wiggins, "and Jones ain't him."

Pilar disregarded Wiggins's statement and addressed Ozzie directly. "What you may not know is that Indigo Jones was approached by that rope salesman. He wanted to hire him and his family to do some big job, a theft. Irma said Indigo wanted to do it, but the rest of the family refused."

Ozzie nodded. "Yes, we know. That's how Indigo Jones knew the rope salesman, Orlando Vile. He was offered the job first." Ozzie bit into his sausage and bean roll. "Why have you come looking for us?" he asked, swallowing.

"Now that there is a murder investigation, the police have closed down the circus. I want to help you."

The boys began to jeer, and Wiggins threw up his hands.

Ozzie waited for silence, then spoke, "I am afraid you have found us at a bad time." He pointed to Wiggins and Rohan. "We have been engaged by Mr. Holmes tonight. He was specific in his instructions. He wants three *boys* to meet him. We will be leaving shortly."

Pilar looked at the other boys. "I am sure he wouldn't mind a fourth assistant," she said.

"Mr. Holmes is our boss, so we do what he says," Wiggins told her.

"It wouldn't be right to bring others along," Ozzie said sympathetically. "I am afraid your involvement in this case is over."

"Has anyone even discovered what happened to Penelope?" Pilar asked.

Ozzie and Wiggins shook their heads.

"I bet no one cares." Pilar buried her face in her hands.

"We're sorry. But I am sure when Mr. Holmes solves the case, he will also have the answer to her fate." Ozzie looked at Wiggins and Rohan. "Boys, we better get going."

Wiggins studied Ozzie. He had devoured two sausage and bean rolls and appeared to be himself again. With his clean shirt on, the wound seemed like a distant memory. Besides, Wiggins knew that once Ozzie had made up his mind about something, there was no stopping him. And he had definitely made up his mind about going to meet Master.

Wiggins nodded to Elliot. "You're in charge while we're gone. Just keep quiet and everything will be all right."

Elliot nodded, wiping his mouth. Then he walked over and climbed up into the coach.

Wiggins turned to Pilar. "It's late for you to be wanderin' about alone. You can stay here if you like, and when we get back, we'll figure a way to get you home."

Pilar, who seemed to have deflated with disappointment, thanked him, but left the Castle without a word.

Ozzie asked Wiggins, "Will she be all right?"

"She looks like she could take care of herself better than this lot," he said, smiling and gesturing to the rest of the gang.

Alfie had stationed himself in front of a small peephole that was located on the main doors to the factory. "There's a hackney waitin' outside."

"I guess Master wants us to ride first-class," said Wiggins.

"More likely he doesn't want us to be late," said Ozzie.

Stealthily, the three boys exited the factory and slipped out of the alley and around to the hackney cab. The driver gave them a nod as they opened the door and climbed into the compartment. Then the cab sped down the street with the boys stretched out comfortably on the cushioned seats.

As they rode through the mist, the buildings flipped by and a lone star pulsed in the darkness. The anticipation of what was to come filled the boys with excitement.

CHAPTER EIGHTEEN
The Irregulars arrive at the docks

The street was desolate, lit only by occasional beams of moonlight. The clopping of the horse cab had faded, and as the boys walked toward the docks, they gazed quietly over their shoulders. None of them was familiar with the area.

Wiggins stopped and looked longingly in the direction from which they had come. A part of him wished he was back at the Castle playing cards with the boys. The loneliness of his childhood clutched him – the endless nights he'd spent awake and afraid, huddled in cold doorways – flashing in his mind like a lightning storm. A sorrowful wind nosed his ankles, and he thought he heard footsteps behind him. He turned anxiously, but saw no one. "Give me a crowd and a riot over this. It'll give ya the collywobbles," he whispered.

The street the boys headed down emptied onto a vast dock some ten or fifteen feet above the Thames. A row of wooden buildings ran along the land side; pylons, crates, and barrels were scattered along the riverside.

When the wind blew, the river rose up and smacked the dock. Rohan looked down. He thought of his father's fishing boat disappearing in the vast swells of the North Sea. Rohan shuddered and moved away from the edge of the dock. He had grown to hate all bodies of water.

Ozzie was uncomfortable, too. His stitches burned, and the heavy fog felt oppressive. Crumbly's plan to chain him up every night would make apprenticing at the shop even more intolerable. And he couldn't help but dwell on the fact he'd had no luck locating his great-aunt Agatha. He was dubious that the letter he planned to post yet again would ever reach her. Everything suddenly seemed beyond his control. With all these dark thoughts preying upon his mind, even the desolate docks became a welcome distraction, as was the company of friends.

The dock creaked, and water lapped fitfully against the pylons. The wind blew sharply, which caused the clouds to clear a bit. Ozzie looked at the scrap of paper Holmes had

With all these dark thoughts preying upon his mind, even the desolate docks became a welcome distraction, as was the company of friends.

given the carriage driver, with the directions to the address of their meeting spot.

As they crept along, Ozzie examined the facades, finally stopping before a dilapidated building. It stood on a corner of the dock and a small street. Two steps led up to the door. The windows were dark. "This is it," he said.

Hesitantly, the boys climbed the steps. Ozzie was about to knock when, out of the corner of his eye, he saw a gloved hand on Wiggins's shoulder and felt one on his own. The boys jumped, and Wiggins cried out.

"Hello," a familiar voice said.

The boys spun around.

"Sorry to have alarmed you." Pilar grinned in the moonlight.

"What are you doing here?" Ozzie said in a stern whisper. This girl had a knack for materializing out of nowhere, he thought. Did that go hand in hand with fortune-telling?

"You're mad," Wiggins declared, regaining his composure.

Rohan was too stunned to speak.

"You must go," Wiggins insisted.

"I have nowhere to go. I arrived on the back of your

cab. I don't know my way home from here." Pilar feigned helplessness.

As the boys argued with her, her expression changed from slightly amused to frightened.

The boys spun around to see the door behind them open. A sailor, with only one eye, stood in the doorway. A hideous scar snaked down his face where the other eye used to be. The man was tall and lean and wore a striped shirt open in a V at the neck, dark wool pants, and a sailor's cap. He scanned the dock and down the street with his one good eye.

"Who are ye?" he demanded in a low, gritty voice. His eye pierced them. "Disturbing the peace on me dock, I should toss you in the river!" He grabbed Ozzie and Wiggins by the front of their collars and yanked them inside with surprising strength. Before Rohan and Pilar could escape, he grabbed them, too.

Once inside, the sailor lifted a lantern from the floor, saying, "Follow me, and one of ye latch the door!" But the sailor's voice had changed, and Ozzie and Wiggins recognized it.

"Master?" they said.

Holmes turned and winked. "Quiet now, and come."

Relieved, the four followed Holmes up the stairs to a large, empty room with two windows facing the buildings across the street. A lone lamp lit the street below, and the dock could be seen off to the right.

Holmes instructed them to line up. Pilar rolled her eyes at the request but complied.

Holmes paced the line. "I'm sorry if I frightened you. But you know my methods. And disguises can be essential."

The boys nodded solemnly.

Stopping before Wiggins, Holmes continued, "You are timely and your selection of companions wise. But who is the Gypsy girl? And more important, who showed the bad judgment of bringing her along?"

Before Wiggins could answer, Pilar said, "I prefer to be addressed directly, sir. My name is Pilar Ana Maria Reina de la Vega. I work in the circus, and your boys would have been lost there if it wasn't for me. I followed them here; it wasn't their idea. And pardon me, but I don't like the way you say *Gypsy*." Pilar looked directly up at Holmes as she spoke.

Holmes muttered, "A little Irene Adler. And why are you here, young lady?"

"I can help."

Holmes dismissed the offer with a wave of his hand. He removed his sailor's cap, proceeded to the windows, and looked out. "With some luck, my friends, tonight will be a fruitful one. I have learned from one of my sources that Orlando Vile often conducts business in the building across the way. I plan to confront him. You are to survey the docks so I know how he arrives and, if he manages to escape me, what path he takes. That is your assignment."

Holmes turned and faced the Irregulars, his face as solemn as Wiggins had ever seen. "We are dealing with a man who will murder anyone who poses even a minimal threat. You are not to approach him under any circumstance. He may not be alone, and his cohorts are among the most dangerous men in London. I reiterate, you are to observe, that is all."

Never before had Master sounded so grave.

"Yes, Mr. Holmes," Wiggins answered for the group.

From inside his shirt, Holmes pulled three yeoman's whistles, hanging from lanyards. He handed one to each of the boys. "If by some misfortune, you find yourselves in harm's way, blow the whistle. If you see Vile escaping, do the same. Osgood, station yourself down the dock in the direction from which you came. Rohan, you are to go up the dock in the other direction. Wiggins, stay on this street, a few buildings aWay. Hide yourselves well. Remember, you are not to be seen."

Holmes paced the room. "I will conduct surveillance from here and then act on the circumstances as they present themselves. Any questions?"

"What am I to do?" Pilar asked.

Holmes sighed with some annoyance. "I did not anticipate your involvement, so you will remain with me."

Pilar crossed her arms, and a scowl formed on her face. "But —"

Holmes cleared his throat. "Boys, you may be waiting for some time. Be patient and alert. Become one with your surroundings. Remember, the key to surveillance is more than not being seen; no one should even imagine you are watching. Your very existence should be unknown.

"I will summon you at the right time. If something unfortunate befalls me, find Watson back at Baker Street. He will know how to proceed. Now please, take your positions."

CHAPTER NINETEEN
Surveillance on the docks

A gray mist blew in across the water, and visibility was patchy. Ozzie crouched behind a stack of crates. The fetid fish odor of the River Thames turned his stomach. He began to sweat, and his head ached. Would he vomit during his biggest assignment?

A face-to-face confrontation with Vile was preferable to another hour sitting on the docks, he decided. He knew Holmes had warned them against such recklessness. But what had he to lose? One of his dark moods overtook him.

For the past few minutes, a hum had been coming down the river, the volume increasing with time to a rumble and clank. A steam launch, Ozzie determined. Stealthily, he positioned himself on the dock near a logical place for the launch to land. Through the mist, he caught occasional glimpses of it.

But when the mist suddenly thickened into a dense yellow fog, Ozzie lost sight of the launch. As it came up alongside the dock, he could hear the roar of the engine, slowly waning to a clatter and hiss. It was eerie not being able to see something just a few feet below you.

Was it possible that the fog was thickening still? Ozzie held up a hand in front of his face. It appeared and vanished with a breath of wind.

Ozzie peered over the edge of the dock and waited for the next breeze to clear the air. The launch had landed beside a small platform at water level. The driver wore a long wool coat and a top hat. Ozzie noted that he seemed too dressed up for his surroundings. He didn't look like a riverboat driver.

Wasn't that what Wiggins told him Barboza had said about the rope salesman? That he didn't seem quite right for his trade?

It must be Orlando Vile! Ozzie realized, fear and exhilaration dueling inside him.

On the platform next to the launch, a stocky hunchbacked man tied down the lines. His arms bulged with muscles, and he moved with the stride and bounce of a gorilla. His broad chIn jutted forward in an extended under bite. His face and hands were streaked with soot markings from stoking the boiler of the launch.

After he finished tying off the lines, the hunchback swung himself back into the boat. Vile gestured to him and then climbed over the side and ascended the ladder to the main dock. Over his shoulder he carried a large, square satchel.

Ozzie moved silently to a hidden vantage point and watched Vile climb up onto the dock. A patch of moonlight illuminated Vile's face — pinched and pockmarked, with a mustache forking downward on either side of his mouth.

By the way Vile moved, Ozzie could tell that the satchel was heavy. A diary used by queens and kings for the last two centuries would have to be large and heavy, Ozzie reasoned. What else could be inside but *The Stuart Chronicle*!

Vile stopped just a few feet from Ozzie. He struck a match and lit a cigar. Then he swaggered down the dock toward Holmes and the others. Ozzie followed.

Vile continued another three hundred feet to the end of the dock, past the building where Holmes and Pilar watched. He leaned back against a barrel, smoked his cigar, and scanned the area.

Ozzie moved silently to a hidden vantage point....

Like a bloodhound, Ozzie trailed the smell of cigar smoke, then crouched behind some debris stacked on the dock. The glow of Vile's cigar pierced the fog. Ozzie could just make out the silhouette of his fiendish frame. Ozzie's stitches began to throb, but he sat quietly and observed.

Meanwhile, Wiggins sat anxiously on an overturned bucket, next to a three-step stoop, tossing crumbs of bread to Shirley. He was glad he'd brought her along for company. The worst part of surveillance was waiting. At least on the busy city streets you could watch the crowd or eavesdrop on interesting conversations. But here on the docks, nothing lived and the silence was eerie and overwhelming. Again, the friendlessness of Wiggins's early days as an orphan crept into his mind and made him shudder. He couldn't help but recall Pilar's warning earlier that day: "Your safety is not guaranteed. Remain as a group and you may survive. Act alone and you will surely die." Well, all three boys were alone now, Wiggins thought nervously.

"Come, Shirley," he whispered, and when the ferret scurried over, he picked her up and held her close.

From nowhere, a two-horse brougham appeared and shot through the fog down the street. Its horses galloped almost angrily, giving the whole apparatus an unearthly air. Wiggins ducked behind a stoop and watched it pass.

The brougham came to a sudden halt in front of a building directly across from the one where Holmes and Pilar were stationed. Wiggins crept down the street for a closer look.

Crouched inside a damp barrel, Rohan held his breath. Cigar smoke wafted down, and he feared he might cough. When he dared to peer upward, he saw the shoulder of a man, leaning against the barrel. He prayed the man would not look down.

A few feet away, Ozzie heard the carriage on the street. Better to return to the launch, he decided, only to see Vile begin walking toward him.

From the second-story window, Holmes and Pilar observed the brougham.

"Our position isn't very good," Pilar said, looking up at Holmes.

They had a side view of the brougham. The driver stepped down and let the passenger out on the opposite side, which was blocked from their view.

Holmes stared at Pilar with unspoken annoyance and then back out the window. "What occurs in the building across from us is the key, young lady, not what occurs on the street."

They watched Vile appear from down the dock, carrying a particularly heavy portmanteau, and then disappear behind the brougham.

"Blast it! We cannot see them," barked Holmes.

Pilar gazed at him, trying hard to contain the very slightest of triumphant smiles.

CHAPTER TWENTY
A stranger appears

Wiggins worked his way toward the brougham, keeping close to the building and out of the moonlight. Alongside the carriage stood the driver. Next to him was a tall, gaunt man with a high, domed forehead, wearing a cape and carrying a satchel; and another man, wearing a top hat, smoking a cigar, and also carrying a satchel. The two men with satchels nodded to each other and shook hands. The cigar smoker removed a key from his pocket and opened the door to the building. Leaving the driver to guard the carriage, the two men entered.

As Wiggins backed away, he disrupted a tin can in the street. The brougham driver swung around and began to take giant strides toward him.

*   *   *

Ozzie had managed to evade Vile and was now repositioned on the dock. He watched the hunchback shovel coal into the launch's burner. Vile must be planning to leave by launch, Ozzie decided, otherwise the boat would not be idling.

"You are not to approach him under any circumstance. . . ." Holmes's warning echoed in Ozzie's mind. But there were no other boats on the river. And if Holmes did not stop Vile before he reached the dock, there would be no way to catch him.

Ozzie spotted a fishnet draped over some boxes across from him. He remembered seeing a block and tackle down a ways. A plan began to form in his mind as he scurried to find them.

Wiggins ran silently away from the brougham driver. A few buildings down the street, he crouched in a doorway. Moonlight illuminated the outline of the driver, who, seeing nothing but dense fog and thick, black night, returned to the carriage.

The gaslights on the second floor of the building across the street lit up the room so that Holmes and Pilar could see the two men. Vile faced the window. The other man, tall and narrow, had his back to them. Holmes pulled out a pair of field glasses and observed.

"May I use them?" Pilar asked.

"Young Lady, this is not a game. What occurs in that room is the key to this case. I must observe everything."

"I can read lips."

Holmes studied Pilar, then handed her the glasses. "We've no time to waste."

Pilar held the glasses up to her eyes and peered out the window. "I cannot see the tall man's face, but Vile is saying, 'Things went well during the job, except at the end. Cesar Zalinda was about to step down from the rope when a tremendous wind blew'— oh, I missed some words . . . wait, now he's saying, 'He hit the top of the fence and fell to the ground.' He's pausing now. The other man must be speaking."

"Keep watching," Holmes instructed.

"Vile is talking again. 'It would not have been so bad, but the other three were very upset, and the girl on lookout started screaming. Of course there were guards all around, so I silenced her. Permanently. The Zalindas panicked. It was

"*I need you to concentrate on what is being said. The crime involves more than just the Zalindas' and Penelope's deaths.*"

all I could do to load the bodies of Cesar and the girl into the coach and ride off. I know it was sloppy work, dumping the bodies in the river, but it was only me and those three mad tightrope walkers.'" Pilar's voice cracked on the last words.

She stopped and looked at Holmes. "He did it, didn't he? He killed Penelope and dumped her and Cesar in the Thames."

Holmes nodded gravely.

"Why are we standing here? Let's do something!"

Holmes watched the window and explained calmly, "I need you to concentrate on what is being said. The crime involves more than just the Zalindas' and Penelope's deaths. Much more is at stake here. We will ensure that justice is done, but —"

Holmes broke off mid-sentence. "What's that? What's that?"

Pilar lifted the field glasses. Vile dropped his satchel to the floor and held up a large book, its cover shiny and sparkling. The tall man with his back to the window stepped forward and took the book from Vile. He turned so that his profile was lit by the gas lamps. He held the book in his palms like an offering. He said two words, which Pilar repeated: "'Precious history.'"

Holmes stood in a slight trance, looking at the tall man, now facing them. He was gaunt, with sunken eyes and a domed forehead, giving the general impression of a reptile.

Though Holmes had never seen him before, he knew him instantly. Under his breath, he said, "Moriarty."

Rubbing his hands together, he muttered, "Of course. Only the Napoleon of Crime himself could be responsible. Who else but Moriarty would have the skill and audacity to steal the *Chronicle*?"

Pilar repeated Moriarty's words. "'The diary of the monarchs. Look at this cover — solid gold, with the brocade of rubies and sapphires. The value of such a book, and most important, the secrets it contains, is immeasurable!'"

Holmes paced the floor. "Yes . . . only the *Chronicle* could draw him from his web. Only a mind as brilliant as his could confirm its existence and appropriate it. This is a fine opportunity indeed."

Hearing Holmes, Pilar put down the field glasses and watched him.

"Keep your eyes on the *Chronicle!*" he ordered.

Startled, Pilar looked through the glasses again, but the two men were lifting their satchels. "The book is gone," she said, disbelieving.

"No matter," Holmes said with resignation. He put his sailor's cap back on and instructed Pilar, "Whatever happens, remain here. I or one of the boys will come for you. You have done well."

Then, with a flourish, he exited the room.

CHAPTER TWENTY-ONE
The confrontations

O zzie threw an old lantern down on the launch, shattering it across the bow. The hunchback swung out of the boat and, in one leap, was climbing up the ladder. Fear coursed through Ozzie's frail body, but he stood facing the man from ten paces away as he stepped up onto the dock. The hunchback's broad feet landed squarely on the fishing net that Ozzie had lain out.

Yes, Ozzie thought. He turned and ran, holding the rope. The sudden movement caused his stitches to burn and he felt a knifelike pain down his side.

A patch of fog blew in, creating a thick curtain between Ozzie and the hunchback.

Ozzie tugged with all his might on the rope. Just as he'd hoped, the fishing net flew up around the hunchback and bagged him. He growled and cursed as he fought the net.

His side aching, Ozzie managed to wrap the rope around a nearby post, keeping hold of the end.

The hunchback was so crazed with ire that he swung in all directions, fighting the net, and propelled himself over the side of the dock. The rope jolted, yanking Ozzie forward before he was able to steady himself and tie it off.

As he did so, Ozzie heard a thud. He looked over the edge of the dock and saw the hunchback hanging unconscious.

Meanwhile, Holmes staggered over to the brougham. With a drunken slur, he said, "What a fancy carriage to be sittin' on me dock! Oh, what do I see now, gentlemen. . . ."

Vile and Moriarty turned, and the brougham driver approached Holmes menacingly. Holmes feigned fright. Looking at the driver, he said, "I just wants to speak with the gentlemen."

Moriarty smirked and waved off his driver. "What is your business?" he asked.

"I'd like to be paid a small tax for using me dock."

Vile yelled, "Enough!" and tossed a handful of coins at Holmes.

Holmes ignored them and pointed to Moriarty. "What a

fine bag you have there, governor. I could use that for me important papers."

Vile pulled a large knife from inside his coat and lunged toward Holmes.

Brandishing his revolver, Holmes said in a more sober voice, "Put down the cheese cutter, mate, or you'll be floatin' in the river before morn'."

Reluctantly, Vile dropped the knife.

Holmes looked at Moriarty holding his briefcase and, without a word, nodded to the street.

Moriarty hesitated, but finally put down the bag.

Holmes motioned to Vile to drop his satchel as well. Then, in his own voice, he called out, "Wiggins!"

Wiggins stepped out from the doorway.

"Gather these satchels and then disappear please."

"We're being held up by a bunch of beggars!" Vile yelled incredulously.

But Moriarty, observing Holmes, wrinkled his heavy brow in recognition. "You!"

Swiftly, Wiggins lifted the bags, looked at Holmes, and ran off.

Suddenly Moriarty's driver knocked Holmes down, sending his gun flying into the street.

"Finally, you oaf!" Vile yelled as he ran for the gun.

Holmes sprang up and gave chase. Beating Vile to the gun, he kicked it into the darkness.

Moriarty climbed into the carriage. The driver had pursued Holmes and threw him down again before jumping into the carriage.

Holmes managed to blow his yeoman's whistle as the carriage drove off. Vile, who was still searching for the gun, fled down the dock.

When four officers from Scotland Yard ran down the street in response to Holmes's whistle, Holmes pointed a few of them in the direction of Vile. Then he raced to catch the brougham and hopped onto the side. The driver whipped him. Dodging, Holmes climbed up to the driver's seat. The two men struggled as the carriage swung around, out of controL.

Some fifty yards away, Vile climbed down to his launch. The engine rattled high, but the hunchback was nowhere to be seen. Vile untied the bowline and hopped into the boat as it bobbed out into the river.

But just before he snapped the engine into gear, it died. That was when he noticed for the first time that the coal pile was gone. With the engine quiet, he heard a soft moaning coming from beneath the dock. "'Twas the skinny lad who done this, sir . . . oh, me head, me head . . ."

A clearing in the fog revealed the hunchback, wrapped in a fishing net, hanging next to the pylons beneath the dock.

Vile exclaimed, "What the —"

"Good evening, sir," Ozzie said, stepping forward and tugging a hidden line. The rope was tied to the dock on one end and to the stern of the launch on the other. "I guess your moonlight ride is about to end."

Vile cursed and attempted to cut the line just as another launch appeared, carrying three policemen. Vile looked at them and then at Ozzie. "You won't get away with this, you bloody little scoundrel. Your life is over!"

Holmes clung with one hand from the edge of the carriage as the driver attempted to kick him off. The carriage had turned

180 degrees, and the horses now ran headlong down the dock toward the water.

Poking his head out of the barrel, Rohan saw the coach racing toward him with Holmes barely holding on. Rohan jumped out and lifted the barrel over his head. With all his strength, he hurled it at the driver. The barrel hit him clean in the shoulder, knocking him off the carriage and onto the ground with a dull thud.

Holmes pulled himself onto the carriage and grabbed the reins, but the horses were too spooked to be controlled.

Moriarty still had not emerged from the brougham's compartment.

Holmes disconnected the carriage from the horses, and the frightened animals turned and ran off into the fog. The carriage, still moving from the momentum of the horses, headed toward the water. Holmes struggled with the brake lever, but it wouldn't lock.

Just before the carriage reached the edge of the dock, he leapt off. The carriage flew into the water and sank quickly.

Moriarty did not surface.

Holmes pulled himself onto the carriage and grabbed the reins,
but the horses were too spooked to be controlled.

CHAPTER TWENTY-TWO
Holmes and the Irregulars inform Scotland Yard

H olmes, the Irregulars, and members of Scotland Yard met inside the building Holmes and Pilar had used for surveillance. The two satchels sat with an air of victory on the floor between them.

Inspector Lestrade questioned Holmes while Wiggins, Pilar, and Rohan gave Ozzie a fresh tourniquet.

"Mr. Holmes you have explained, er, rather we have discussed what has occurred, but I would expect more information."

"Inspector, bring in Orlando Vile, and you will learn all the additional details you require."

Moments later, two officers led Vile, in handcuffs, into the room.

Vile moved violently. "You have nothing on me!" Eyeing Holmes, he barked, "Who are you?"

"I am Sherlock Holmes, and I am quite familiar with the specifics of your crimes over the past three days, so if you would, kindly provide us with a few details that I wish to confirm."

With a bitter smile, Vile said, "Holmes the meddler, I've heard of you, and as far as I can see, you know nothing."

Holmes proceeded to summarize how Vile engaged the Zalindas to steal *The Stuart Chronicle* from Buckingham Palace.

Vile scoffed. "You have no proof."

"You should consider cooperating. It is your only chance to avoid the harshest criminal charges, since you are guilty of the murders of the Zalindas and Penelope as well as the theft of *The Stuart Chronicle*, which could be considered treason. As far as I can see, you have a future appointment with the gallows. I should add that Inspector Lestrade has recently arrested two maids who were formerly employed at Buckingham Palace; both will testify they were accomplices to a theft that you committed. My first inquiry is, how did Cesar Zalinda die?" Holmes glanced in Pilar's direction and nodded.

Vile said nothing.

"You should consider cooperating. It is your only chance to avoid the harshest criminal charges...."

"Very well," said Holmes. "I shall tell what happened. After learning the location of the *Chronicle* from one of the maids, you arranged for the other to be stationed on the second floor of the north side of the palace. She lowered a line to one of the Zalindas, who ran across the courtyard, pulling the tightrope behind him. The same Zalinda scaled the building and set the tightrope, which was strung from the perimeter fence to the second-floor window. It was a particularly dark and foggy night, and the three remaining Zalindas crossed unseen over the palace courtyard, directly above the unsuspecting guards. They made a human tower from the rope up to the third floor, allowing the fourth Zalinda to climb them and to lift the *Chronicle* from Her Majesty's study undetected.

"The only complication occurred as they were leaving. As the Zalindas walked the tightrope back across the courtyard, a heavy wind began to blow, which is the fear of every tightrope walker. They made it back to the fence and the first three brothers managed to dismount. But the wind grew stronger, and the rope began to sway. The remaining brother, Cesar, lost his footing and fell on top of the fence and then to the ground. It is sadly ironic that such a small fall would cause the death of a man accustomed to working at great heights.

"Penelope, who'd been stationed as lookout, began to wail when Cesar landed at her feet. You, Mr. Vile, jumped out of the waiting carriage and attempted to quiet her. In your zealousness, you strangled the poor young woman. You then instructed the Zalindas to load Cesar's and Penelope's bodies into the carriage. The tightrope was released from the palace by the maid and collected by the Zalindas so that there was no evidence of the break-in. You then disposed of Cesar's and Penelope's bodies in the Thames."

Ozzie looked at Pilar, standing beside him. She had tears in her eyes.

Holmes continued. "The final step of the plan was carried out by you alone. The next day, you sabotaged the Zalindas' tightrope with this." From his pocket, Holmes pulled the pin Wiggins had discovered and opened it, revealing the razor center.

"Your motive was simple. Eliminate all witnesses to the theft of *The StuaRt Chronicle*."

Holmes paused and looked directly at Vile. "And there was Professor Moriarty himself, the Napoleon of Crime.

Only a mind as logical as his could plan such a carefully thought-out crime. Only he could learn of the existence of *The Stuart Chronicle* and know how to fully exploit it."

Vile scoffed again. "Moriarty would not have succeeded if not for me. The professor was a great man, but I planned this caper. He learned of the existence of the *Chronicle* and left the rest to me."

"You have all that, Inspector?" Holmes said, turning to Lestrade, who was taking notes.

"Yes, Mr. Holmes, I do," Lestrade answered.

"Though we didn't capture Moriarty, we do have the *Chronicle*." Holmes waved Wiggins over and asked for Moriarty's satchel. With great pride, Wiggins opened it and looked inside. "What —?" he exclaimed, turning to Holmes dumbstruck. Inside was only a brick.

Vile laughed maniacally.

Surprised, Holmes reached for Vile's satchel, but it was empty.

"He took it with him, Holmes. Even in death, the professor outfoxed you," Vile gloated. "You are right that he knew the value of the *Chronicle*, and he insisted on keeping it on his person for safety reasons. Though I thought he was being extreme, he was right as always. You may have driven him to the bottom of the Thames, Holmes, but he took *The Stuart Chronicle* with him."

As the officers led Vile away, his devilish laugh echoed through the room.

Dejected, Holmes turned to Lestrade. "Inspector, I suggest you obtain a few boats and start trolling the river for Moriarty and the *Chronicle* at first daylight."

He looked to the Irregulars and Pilar. "We are finished here."

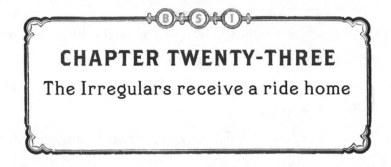

CHAPTER TWENTY-THREE
The Irregulars receive a ride home

A police carriage drove Holmes, Ozzie, Pilar, Wiggins, and Rohan back to Baker Street. Ozzie wanted to question Holmes about the crime and what would happen to Vile and to hear more about *The Stuart Chronicle*. But seeing the great detective lost in thought, humming softly to himself, Ozzie refrained.

"My organization," Holmes said, breaking his trance. "It was a miscalculation on my part not to save the *Chronicle*, but you all did exemplary work. We cannot forget that Professor Moriarty, the most dangerous man in all of England, appears to be dead. He will not easily be replaced.

"As usual, Wiggins, you were reliable, timely, and brought the right companions. You kept a close and careful watch and appeared and disappeared with the satchels like a professional thief."

"We cannot forget that Professor Moriarty, the most dangerous man in all of England, appears to be dead. He will not easily be replaced."

Wiggins nodded proudly.

Holmes then addressed Rohan. "I would not be sitting here if you had not taken care of Moriarty's driver with that barrel. As I clung with one hand from the coach, I realized that if he succeeded in kicking me off, I would have fallen beneath the carriage wheels and likely been rent in two."

Rohan bowed his head respectfully. "It was an honor, sir."

Holmes smiled at Pilar. "Your confidence and ability make you an asset on any surveillance. I have never found so useful a person of your sex."

The boys looked at one another surprised; they had never heard Master compliment a female.

Pilar tried to conceal her happiness.

Holmes then looked at Ozzie. "In spite of my warning not to approach Vile, in this situation you exercised good judgment. I doubt Scotland Yard's best could have single-handedly captured him and his hunchback assistant. Pray, tell us how you managed that."

Ozzie explained. "After netting the hunchback, I climbed down to the steam launch and turned up the boiler so all the fuel would burn off quickly. I then dumped the remaining fuel over the side of the boat, tied another line off the stern, and ran it inconspicuously through the water to a less visible portion of the dock. In this way, when Vile came down and cast off, he was far from shore before he realized the boat was still tied to the dock. With no fuel in the launch, I thought I had him, but if it wasn't for Scotland Yard, Vile would probably have gotten away."

Holmes said, proudly, "You can take credit for the capture of those two. It amazes me that you did so nonviolently. You show promisE."

Ozzie felt his cheeks flush.

As the carriage turned onto Baker Street, Holmes continued, "I must impress upon all of you the need for confidentiality with respect to *The Stuart Chronicle*. You are not to utter a word of what you know. The matter is of the utmost secrecy — and your knowledge of it could put you in danger. It is for this reason that I did not involve Watson more in this case. I feared he would write about it."

The boys and Pilar all agreed to keep *The Stuart Chronicle* a secret.

"Lastly," Holmes said, smiling, "you must learn that satisfaction from doing one's work well is what matters most. But, compensation for one's work is also important." Holmes handed each of them two one-pound notes, the most money the boys had ever earned. It was enough, Ozzie realized with a start, to go in search of Great-aunt Agatha.

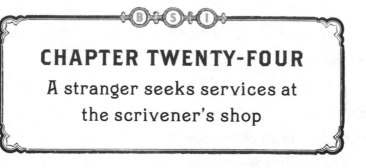

CHAPTER TWENTY-FOUR
A stranger seeks services at
the scrivener's shop

W hen the police carriage arrived at Baker Street, they were all weary, even Holmes. They said their good-byes, and Holmes headed upstairs to inform Watson of the night's events. Wiggins and Rohan returned to the carriage factory, and Ozzie to the scrivener's shop. Before the police coach drove her home, Pilar made Ozzie promise that he'd come visit her at the circus grounds.

It was now shortly before dawn. Ozzie entered the shop, too tired to care what Crumbly would think. He turned the key in the door of the storage room, dove onto his pallet, and fell asleep immediately.

A few hours later, Ozzie was awoken by talking in the front room. As he peered through the doorway, Ozzie saw Crumbly and a tall, well-dressed gentleman with a dominant forehead talking quietly by one of the desks. The man stopped and stared at Ozzie. Something in his eyes and the lines around his mouth made Ozzie uncomfortable.

Crumbly turned and, seeing Ozzie, frowned. But he controlled his anger and waved Ozzie over. "There he is, sir. The best forger in all of London."

Hesitantly, Ozzie approached.

The man looked at Crumbly and said, "You entrust your work to a boy?"

Crumbly pulled a piece of paper from the desk drawer and placed it on the desk. "Write a sentence, sir."

The man picked up a quill and wrote.

Ozzie sat on the stool at the table and copied the line directly beneath it in a swift cursive.

The man watched and then compared. He smiled. "It is identical. You do fine work, lad."

The gentleman spoke pleasantly enough, but still, there was something about his demeanor that frightened Ozzie.

The man opened his cape. A large package wrapped in oilskin was strapped to his chest. He removed it and withdrew a jewel-encrusted book, which he placed on the table.

At the sight of the gold-and-jewel-covered volume, Crumbly stood speechless, his mouth hanging slack.

Ozzie shivered and blinked. He couldn't believe it. The book had to be *The Stuart Chronicle*. Which meant that the man standing before him was Professor Moriarty. Moriarty was alive!

Crumbly asked, "If you don't mind me askin', what is it, Professor?"

Moriarty said, "I do mind. Don't ask questions. Your job does not require additional information. The paper in this is some two hundred years old; every detail must be perfect."

"Don't you worry, sir," said Crumbly. "We have reams of paper from that era and know the exact type of inks used. We can reproduce everything identically, down to the gold trim. But what of the cover?"

"We have others working on the cover. That is not your concern."

Ozzie drew closer to the *Chronicle* and, as the two men spoke, thumbed through it. The ancient book drew him in instantly. The handwriting was masterful and ornate, the pages as long as his arm and of fine, thick paper. The aura of other eras emanated from it.

"We'll need the largest quills, with gold nubs," Ozzie said, paging carefully through the *Chronicle*. "This ink is

The ancient book drew him in instantly.

better than the best. We'll have to create some special blend, India with gold leaf. Though old, the book is in immaculate condition. The duplicate will require top-quality paper. There must be eight hundred written pages here by over ten different authors. This will take some time."

Surprised by Ozzie's examination, Moriarty addressed him directly. "Boy, if your work impresses me as much as you have, you may find a position with my organization. And I assure you, the pay is far more generous than whatever this gnome pays you. But you have quite a fair amount of work to do first." Moriarty then turned to Crumbly. "I'll need the book copied in five days."

The smile left Crumbly's face, and he swung his short, beefy arms nervously. "Professor, the boy is the best, but he would be lucky to finish in two weeks. May I suggest having a second to aid him? I have just the man. We could do twice the work in half the time."

"No," Moriarty said flatly. "I want only the boy." He waved two men in off the street.

"For security reasons, these two will remain with you until the copy is completed. Neither you nor the boy will leave the building during that time. If anything happens to this book, I will hold you both personally responsible. I can't keep my buyer waiting any longer. You have one week, lad, but not a day more."

Turning to Crumbly, Moriarty continued, "I find it hard to believe that a man of your appearance would have such a fine reputation. But that is irrelevant as long as the copy is of the finest quality. If this happens, you will be well compensated. If not, well . . . I'm sure you don't want to dwell on the consequences."

As he exiTed, Moriarty looked at Ozzie and said with something close to sincerity, "Good luck, boy."

CHAPTER TWENTY-FIVE
Wiggins and Pilar call on Holmes

Three days later, Wiggins and Pilar appeared anxiously in Holmes's flat.

"So there was two rough characters in the shop, and Ozzie was writin' away, and he looked up and saw us through the window and started mouthin' and no one could hear him but Pilar saw him doin' it, and she knows what he said, and it was about the *Chronicle*, and he's a prisoner, and those thugs saw us, and one opened the door and started to chase us, and Oz said Moriarty's alive and that it was a book of joy and pleasure, and he kept sayin' 'the eggs,' 'the eggs,' didn't he, like he was goin' bloomin' mad."

"Please, Wiggins, I know you are excited, but kindly sit down before you start to hyperventilate. You look upset as well, señorita. If you please." Holmes motioned to the settee.

Wiggins and Pilar both sat down. Wiggins's hands shook. Pilar's left eye twitched.

"If you could, Wiggins, please take a deep breath and answer my questions."

Wiggins complied, breathing in and out with exaggerated effort.

Holmes sat calmly, a slight smile parting his lips as he puffed on his pipe. Watson watched Wiggins's performance with some amusement as well.

"Let us begin at the beginning," Holmes said. "What compelled you to go to the scrivener's shop?"

"She came to the Castle and said, 'What, he's been gone for three days and you haven't gone to check,' but we did go to check and —"

"Let me help," Pilar interrupted.

Holmes nodded. "If you could, young lady. Our friend Wiggins seems too distressed at Osgood's predicament to make perfect sense."

"I came to visit the boys and learned that Ozzie had not been seen for three days. So Wiggins and I went looking for him at Oxford Scriveners. When we arrived, we peeked in

214

the window and saw Ozzie working at a large desk and two brutish men sitting on either side of him, like guards. Ozzie looked terrible, as though he hadn't slept since we'd last seen him. We tried to get his attention without alerting the guards, but with little luck. Finally, he looked out the window and saw me. He turned his eyes back to his work but mouthed some words, and I read his lips.

"Ozzie said that Moriarty is alive and that he was creating a duplicate of *The Stuart Chronicle* for him. He said that the *Chronicle* was not what it appeared, and Moriarty did not know what he really had." Pilar paused. She seemed truly upset.

"Holmes, Moriarty is alive!" Watson exclaimed.

Holmes continued to smoke his pipe, unsurprised. Watson sat up more attentively and cleared his throat.

"Ozzie then s-s-said . . ." Pilar stammered, and sobbed.

"What did he say?" asked Watson patiently.

"He said it was not a book, but a treasure chest, and that the writing meant nothing. Vile and Moriarty must not have read it. When Moriarty finds out the truth, he'll tear the *Chronicle* apart to find the eggs and do away with Ozzie. Ozzie said there were enough eggs to buy a whole army."

"It is time to plan our next move."

Pilar buried her face in her hands.

"Eggs?" Watson asked quizzically.

Holmes jUmped to his feet and paced the apartment.

"Holmes, what on earth is the girl talking about?"

Holmes kept pacing as if he did not hear Watson.

"Holmes, please tell us what you are thinking," Watson urged.

"Our friend Osgood, in addition to his other abilities, appears to be a master forger and knows a little about history. He's quite right that Moriarty does not know what he has, for if he did, the game would be over by now. It is time to plan our next move."

"The next move should be to save Ozzie," Pilar said, her voice straining.

"Patience. We will save Osgood and recover the *Chronicle*, but we must also trap Moriarty."

"We didn't trap him the last time," Pilar said. "Why take a chance? Something might happen to Ozzie."

"I share your concerns, but nothing will happen to him. I simply need to call off the sale."

"Sale?" inquired Watson.

Holmes grinned as he bent over his desk and wrote a note. "The sale of the *Chronicle*, of course. I was negotiating to buy it from Moriarty."

"What!" Watson, Wiggins, and Pilar exclaimed simultaneously.

Holmes finished writing his note and summoned Billy from downstairs.

"Billy, take this to the telegraph office and have it sent to our friends in Switzerland." Billy nodded to Holmes and the others as he exited the flat.

Holmes then explained. "With the help of some contacts in Geneva, I have been posing as a Swiss rare book collector of questionable reputation by the name of Stocker Bowes. Shortly after the theft of *The Stuart Chronicle*, I convinced Moriarty's people that I, Bowes, was interested in buying it. You can imagine my surprise when I was contacted the day after our night at the docks and told we had a deal. I inferred that both the *Chronicle* and Moriarty had survived the plunge into the Thames. Apparently Moriarty decided to swindle me by selling a bogus copy. In that way, he could keep the *Chronicle* and profit from its sale at the same time. I have just written a note to Moriarty's people indicating that the sale is off. Undoubtedly, Moriarty has shown such an interest in the *Chronicle* that he will attempt to retrieve it immediately from his forgers. When he does, we will be waiting for him."

"What do you make of the eggs that Osgood mentioned? And what does he mean when he says that Moriarty will destroy the *Chronicle*?" Watson asked.

"Let me save one surprise for the end, my friend. Then Osgood may have the pleasure of answering your questions. We have approximately three hours before we need to be at the scrivener's shop. It will take that long for my telegram to reach Switzerland and for my contacts there to forward it back to England and Moriarty. Why not have some lunch before then? I believe Mrs. Hudson has made enough for the four of us."

CHAPTER TWENTY-SIX
Holmes and the Irregulars
save Ozzie

By the end of lunch, Wiggins had recovered from the upset of Ozzie's detention. Food always calmed his nerves, and Mrs. Hudson was a stupendous cook. With his belly full and his spirit renewed, he left 221 B Baker Street and collected the rest of the Irregulars. At Master's direction, he brought them to Oxford Street. By now it was late afternoon, and the sky nearly sparkled a celestial blue, dotted here and there with only a few puffy clouds.

"Okay, boys, I need you to split up," Wiggins said. "Rohan, choose three mates and go sit against the building next to the shop. Elliot, take the rest across the way. As usual, occupy yourselves until you see me signal. Be patient."

"Do we get paid extra if one of us saves Oz?" Alfie asked.

Wiggins tugged Alfie's ear. "Elf, you little wally, if you save Oz, we get Oz back. He's the prize. Any other questions?"

"What are we looking for?" asked Rohan.

"Just keep your mincers open for anyone walkin' in the shop. I'll be over by that hansom cab," Wiggins said, pointing. "That's where Mr. Holmes and Doctor Watson are waitin'."

"And the girl?" said Elliot.

"Pilar is there as well. I'll give you the signal when Master needs us. Now move on."

Wiggins walked past the windows of the shop and saw Ozzie looking down at his desk, copying the *Chronicle*. The two men and Crumbly sat off to the side talking.

Across the street, Holmes sat in the rear of the hansom, dressed as a driver with a long scarf and a canvas hat. He smoked a cigarette. Watson sat in the cab like a passenger, reading a newspaper.

Pilar stood on the street holding a bouquet of flowers, calling, "A rose for your sweetheart, a rose for your sweetheart!" to all those who passed.

By now, Elliot, Alfie, and their group were stationed down the way, as instructed. Wiggins saw them begging for change. Rohan and his group loafed against the wall across the street, acting as if they were too tired to do anything.

Wiggins sat on the sidewalk, in close proximity to the hansom. He tossed out scraps of bread from his pocket and played a game of fetch with Shirley. None of them acknowledged the others' presence.

For a September day in London, the air was remarkably clear and dry. Wiggins comforted himself with the thought that it was too nice a day for anything bad to happen. He continued tossing crumbs to Shirley, and occasionally attempted to get her to jump through a little hoop he had made from some bent wire. From time to time, Pilar would catch Wiggins's eye. Without words, she communicated her concern and impatience.

Then suddenly three four-wheelers came riding down the street side by side at a quick trot. They came to a stop in front of Oxford Scriveners. Wiggins noticed that each carriage was pulled by two black horses and that the coaches were the same in every way. All three drivers even wore identical top hats and gray overcoats and resembled one another in build and demeanor.

Holmes spoke under his breath to Wiggins. "It's the old shell game. Moriarty must suspect us. Signal the boys, Wiggins. This game is over."

Wiggins picked up Shirley and stood. He patted her with exaggerated strokes, then moved her from hand to hand. Both Rohan and Elliot saw the signal and nodded.

Meanwhile, from each of the coaches, a man stepped out. All three strode with a purposeful gait into Crumbly's shop.

A few minutes later, the same men exited. They each carried what appeared to be a large book wrapped in paper and were accompanied by the two men who'd been guarding Ozzie. The drivers climbed back up into the four-wheelers, with the guards following.

"I suppose he expects us to choose who we'll chase. Enough. I have never been a gambler. Wiggins, you and one group of boys follow me. The rest help Watson."

Holmes smacked the reins and the horse, wearing blinders, swung the hansom cab around. Holmes brought it lengthwise to a stop directly in front of all three four-wheelers.

"It's the old shell game."

Watson exited the cab and joined Holmes in the driver's seat. Holmes handed him the reins and instructed, "Stand firm."

Wiggins yelled, "Elliot's crew, spook the horses. Rohan, follow Master."

Elliot, Alfie, and three other boys ran up to the horses harnessed to the four-wheelers, yelling and waving their arms. The horses reared up, and the drivers struggled to steady them.

Wiggins, Pilar, Rohan, and others followed Holmes down an alley running alongside the scrivener's shop. As they turned the corner, they saw another hansom cab waiting directly behind the shop. Ozzie was being dragged out the back door by Crumbly and another man. Crumbly carried *The Stuart Chronicle*. Ozzie looked like the walking dead.

At Holmes's nod, Wiggins and Rohan charged at Crumbly and tackled him.

Pinned to the ground, Crumbly clung like a baby to the *Chronicle*, all the while grunting and yelling, "Off me, you beasts!"

"Release the boy," Holmes told Moriarty's man.

In a panic, he let go of Ozzie and threw a roundhouse punch at Holmes. Holmes ducked and weaved, moving his feet like a boxer. He threw neat, precise jabs at the other man's chin.

During this exchange, Pilar climbed up into the hansom and motioned to Ozzie.

Crumbly was still trying to wrestle Wiggins and Rohan with one arm as he clutched the *Chronicle* with the other. Wiggins and Rohan yanked Crumbly's arms, causing him to release his grasp of the *Chronicle*. In a trice, Ozzie grabbed it.

"You don't look so good, mate," Wiggins told him. "Go on over to Pilar and wait for us."

Ozzie smiled as he held the *Chronicle* before him. "I just need some of your fine cooking, Wiggins, and I'll be back to myself. Give him an extra elbow or two in the ribs for me, will you," he said, looking down at Crumbly. Then he hobbled over to the hansom and climbed up.

Pilar snapped the Reins. "Shall we go for a ride until all this is cleaned up?"

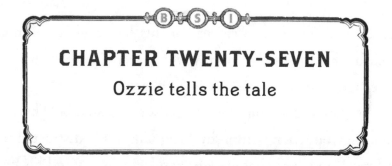

CHAPTER TWENTY-SEVEN
Ozzie tells the tale

Some forty minutes later, Holmes, Watson, and the Irregulars gathered back at the Castle. They sat around the fire pit, with Holmes and Watson resting on wooden crates that Wiggins had pulled over.

Shortly after Ozzie and Pilar arrived back at the scene at the scrivener's shop, police officers had appeared and all those involved in the crime were taken into custody. Moriarty was not among the occupants of the four-wheelers and it was determined that he had likely slipped back into his lair.

Holmes obtained the *Chronicle* from Ozzie and after promising to deliver it to Lestrade at Scotland Yard later that evening and explain everything, he and the Irregulars were permitted to leave.

Now as they revisited the events of the past few hours,

Ozzie held *The Stuart Chronicle* on his lap. Holmes allowed each of the boys a chance to gaze upon the jewel-encrusted cover and turn the ancient, ornate pages.

As they did so, one by one, Ozzie explained, "The eloquent introduction written by King Charles II distracted me at first. You see, it contains his wonderful script and his personal seal. I assumed that the *Chronicle* was as you explained, sir." He looked at Holmes. "A personal record of kings and queens. But I soon realized that it was quite a silly book, filled with nursery rhymes, funny little poems, and songs all written at different times."

Holmes nodded, but Watson looked surprised. "You mean to tell me, Holmes, that you were engaged by the prince of Wales to recover a children's book?"

"Not exactly, Doctor," Ozzie replied. "You can see plainly that the book's cover, of gold and jewels, is of immeasurable value. But this is only a trifle compared with the book's hidden treasure. May I, Mr. Holmes?"

Holmes smiled. "I believe you have earned the right to disclose the surprise to the rest of us."

"I had been copying the *Chronicle* for two days before I

discovered it." Ozzie turned the pages to the middle. Though not noticeable at first, two small loops of cord extended from its binding. Ozzie asked Pilar to hold the cover as he pulled on the loops. The bound pages of the *Chronicle* lifted out from the leather binding, leaving a hollow rectangular space between the front and back covers.

"The binding is hollow," Wiggins said in awe. "Like a long box."

"Exactly," said Ozzie, reaching into the hiding place and removing a stone the size and shape of an egg. Light reflected off it, making it radiate a stunning green.

"An emerald?" Watson said with disbelief.

Ozzie handed it to him and removed two more, identical in shape and size, from the hiding place. He handed one to Holmes and one to Pilar.

"Jewels?" said Wiggins.

"A dozen of them," said Ozzie.

"These must be the largest emeralds in existence," Watson said, still incredulous.

Holmes lifted his up before his eyes. With a slight squint, he said, "You are looking at what most people believe to be simply a fairy tale — the Eggs of Galilee. Possibly the most valuable emeralds in the world. They passed through so many hands that it was never known whether they truly existed. They were last reported in Tangiers some two hundred years ago. Charles II must have acquired them during a particularly fruitful time for the monarchy."

"They are beautiful," said Pilar, turning hers over and over in her hand. "Like a small world."

"I remember learning about KiNg Charles I from my grandfather and how he didn't have enough money to raise an army and that was why he lost the throne," Ozzie said.

Holmes nodded. "Certainly that was one of the reasons. It followed logically that his son, Charles II, after regaining the throne, would take steps to secure his position, but also to ensure he would have funds available for any unexpected events. In this one precious book, he secreted enough jewels to raise an army. Succeeding monarchs must have recognized the practicality of his idea and left the gems hidden in the *Chronicle*. A portable treasure. Apparently the Prince of Wales was so concerned about protecting this secret that he kept it even from me."

"You are looking at what most people believe to be simply a fairy tale—the Eggs of Galilee."

"Incredible," said Watson.

"One of those eggs could make us all kings," said Alfie as he leaned forward to touch Ozzie's.

All the boys shared that same thought as they gazed at the gems.

"Boys, I cannot promise you treasure, but I am certain your services will be appreciated," Holmes told them.

"But what of Moriarty?" Ozzie asked.

"He has undoubtedly sunk back to the center of his web. He will not resurface — unless, of course, the prize is too great to resist."

"And what of Ozzie?" asked Pilar. "He won't have to return to Crumbly, will he?"

Ozzie felt his stomach turn at the thought.

Holmes shook his head. "Jack Crumbly will not only be out of business, but likely jailed. I am afraid, Osgood, your days as a scrivener's — or rather a forger's apprentice are over." Holmes looked about. "It appears, however, that you might find adequate lodgings here."

"Mr. Holmes, we accept all kinds. I suppose we could put up Osgood for some time." Wiggins smiled and punched Ozzie in the shoulder.

The boys cheered, and Ozzie was suddenly so washed with relief and joy that he felt his eyes well up. "Thank you, mates. I'd be honored to call this place home."

With that, Holmes collected the emeralds and replaced them carefully in the spine of *The Stuart Chronicle*. "Undoubtedly, there will be more work ahead of us," Holmes told the boys as he and Watson prepared to leave. "You should all get some rest now." Then, turning to Pilar, he said, "We will arrange a ride home for you."

Pilar sighed, and then gave Wiggins and Ozzie hugs.

"We'll come visit you at the circus," Ozzie said.

"If you don't, I'll find you." Pilar winked as she pulled on her cloak and followed Holmes and Watson out the trapdoor.

Alone once again, the Irregulars gathered their blankets. Wiggins fetched an extra one for Ozzie and laid it out beside his, near the dimly glowing coals. The case of the Zalindas had been exciting, but the gang was exhausted.

"Sing us a tune, won't ya, Wiggins?" Alfie asked sleepily.

As a pearly moon rose over London's West End, he happily obliged.

"While the moon her watch is keeping
All through the night
While the weary world is sleeping
All through the night
O'er thy spirit gently stealing
Visions of delight revealing
Breathes a pure and holy feeling
All through the night.

Angels watching ever round thee
All through the night
In thy slumbers close surround thee
All through the night
They should of all fears disarm thee
No forebodings should alarm thee
They will let no peril harm thee
All through the night."

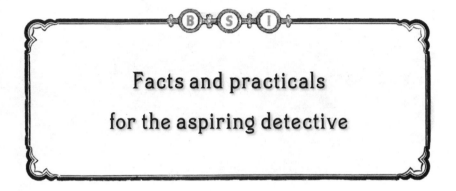

Facts and practicals

for the aspiring detective

CAST OF CHARACTERS

The Baker Street Irregulars

Osgood Manning ("Ozzie")

Wiggins

Rohan

Alfie ("Elf")

Elliot ("Stitch")

Alistair

Barnaby

Fletcher

Simpson

James

Pete

Shem

Shirley, *Wiggins's ferret*

221 B Baker Street

Sherlock Holmes, *Consulting detective*

Dr. John Watson, *Holmes's partner*

Mrs. Hudson, *Holmes and Watson's landlady*

Billy, *Holmes's page*

Circus Folk

Pilar, *Fortune-teller's daughter*

Madam Estrella, *Fortune-teller*

Avalon Barboza (Abel Price), *Ringmaster of the Grand Barboza Circus*

Karlov the Great, *Knife thrower*

Indigo Jones, *Trapeze artist*

Penelope, *Knife thrower's assistant*

Werner Zalinda, *Tightrope walker*

Wilhelm Zalinda, *Tightrope walker*

Wolfgang Zalinda, *Tightrope walker*

Cesar Zalinda, *Tightrope walker*

The Lion Trainer

Angelina and Balina, *Jekyll and Hyde Siamese twins*

Clarence, *Human cannonball*

Big Collar, *Clown*

Floppy Hat (Watty), *Clown*

The Royal Family

Edward, *Prince of Wales*

The Villains

Professor James Moriarty, *"Napoleon of Crime"*

Orlando Vile, *Fourth most dangerous man in London*

Oxford Scriveners

Jack Crumbly, *Proprietor and Ozzie's master*

Frankie, *Master forger*

Police

Inspector Lestrade, *Scotland Yard*

Officer Grey

SLANG GLOSSARY

Page No.	Slang	Translation
21	China plate	*Mate*
21	Bees 'n' honey	*Money*
21	Bow Bells	*The bells of St. Mary-le-Bow Church—it is said that a person born within the sound of the bells is a true Londoner*
27	Rosebuds	*Spuds* (potatoes)
27	Layabout	*Lazy person*
31	Bog	*Toilet*
38	Git	*Stupid person*
40	I've clocked a plod, chase the sun!	*I knocked over a policeman, run!*

Page No.	Slang	Translation
48	Fur coats and no knickers	*To think you are better than you are*
77	Bounder	*Rascal*
85	Chattin' up	*Flirting*
94	Gyppo	*Gypsy*
102	Barmy	*Crazy*
107	Scapa Flow	*Go*
152	Flash flood	*Blood*
166	Collywobbles	*Creeps*
213	Joy and pleasure	*Treasure*
221	Wally	*Idiot*
221	Mincers	*Eyes*

COCKNEY RHYMING SLANG
An explanation and instructions for creating your own

Though a proper Londoner speaks only the Queen's English, other sorts converse in a slang so thick it sounds like a secret code. Such people, born in the East End of London, are called Cockneys. The origins of their original rhyming slang are not clear. Some say it was created by mongers, street merchants who did not want customers to understand their conversations about business. Others say it was created by criminals in jail so they could speak freely in front of the guards. And still others hold that Cockney rhyming slang simply developed as the unique vernacular of London's East End.

Whatever its origins, Cockney rhyming slang can be of immeasurable use to the detective when he or she needs to communicate in code with associates. It is recommended that the novice detective practice with friends or family members before attempting to use the slang on a case. Halted, uncertain speech can be an obvious clue that one is trying to be discreet, and have the opposite effect of exposing one's cover.

Let's try a simple example. Begin by choosing a word, such as "stew." Next, pick a word that rhymes with it: "dew." Then, think of a word or phrase that goes with "dew" to form a natural pairing or phrase: "morning dew." Now, when employing Cockney rhyming slang, instead of saying "stew," you would say "morning dew." For added secrecy, you can shorten this to simply "morning."

Now let's try a whole sentence. Say you are at your auntie's house and she serves you and your brother stew that tastes dreadful. You do not want to be rude, but you would like to share your feelings about the stew with your brother.

First, choose what you want to say in proper English. For example, "The stew tastes like dung."

Next, follow the steps below to come up with words and/or phrases that rhyme with some or most of the words in the sentence.

1) Being that "the" is a rather plain word, we'll let it remain as is.

2) Take the second word: "stew." Using our example above, we'll replace it with the pairing "morning

dew" (because "dew" rhymes with "stew" and "morning" goes with "dew"). But then, to be more discreet, we'll drop the "dew" and just keep "morning."

3) Take the third word, "tastes." What rhymes with it? Bastes? Wastes? Pastes? Let's use "pastes."

4) Now we'll add to it and make it "toothpastes." But, we'll drop "pastes" and keep "tooth."

5) "Like" is rather a plain word, too, so we'll let it remain as is.

6) The last word is "dung." What rhymes with it? Stung? Rung? Tongue? Let's use "tongue."

7) Again, let's add to it and make it a phrase: "tip of my tongue."

So after tasting your auntie's stew, you say to your brother, "The morning tooth like tip of my tongue." Now you have warned him and shared your feelings regarding the ghastly stew, but have not hurt your auntie's feelings.

Again, it is suggested that you try out hundreds of such examples, both written and spoken aloud, in order to hone your skills with this code. Remember, the serious detective must tirelessly practice his or her craft. As Sherlock Holmes said, "I never remember feeling tired by work, though idleness exhausts me completely." ("The Sign of Four")

THE SCIENCE OF DEDUCTION
Sherlock Holmes's mind at work

Undoubtedly, the surest way to learn deduction is by studying an example of the master Sherlock Holmes's powers. This fine bit of work comes from "The Adventure of the Blue Carbuncle," published in The Adventures of Sherlock Holmes *by Sir Arthur Conan Doyle. {The attribution of speakers has been added by the editors.}*

Watson took the tattered object in his hands and turned it over rather ruefully. It was a very ordinary black hat of the usual round shape, hard, and much the worse for wear. The lining had been of red silk, but was a good deal discoloured. There was no maker's name; but, as Holmes had remarked, the initials "H. B." were scrawled upon one side. It was pierced in the brim for a hat-securer, but the elastic was missing. For the rest, it was cracked, exceedingly dusty, and spotted in several places, although there seemed to have been some attempt to hide the discoloured patches by smearing them with ink.

Watson: I can see nothing.

Holmes: On the contrary, Watson, you can see everything. You fail, however, to reason from what you see. You are too timid in drawing your inferences. . . . That the man was highly intellectual is of course obvious upon the face of it, and also that he was fairly well-to-do within the last three years, although he has now fallen upon evil days. He had foresight, but has less now than formerly, pointing to a moral retrogression, which, when taken with the decline of his fortunes, seems to indicate some evil influence, probably drink, at work upon him. This may account also for the obvious fact that his wife has ceased to love him. . . . He has, however, retained some degree of self-respect. . . . He is a man who leads a sedentary life, goes out little, is out of training entirely, is middle-aged, has grizzled hair which he has had cut within the last few days, and which he anoints with lime-cream. These are the more patent facts which are to be deduced from his hat. Also, by the way, that it is extremely improbable that he has gas laid on in his house.

Watson: ... I must confess that I am unable to follow you. For example, how did you deduce that this man was intellectual?

Holmes clapped the hat upon his head. It came right over the forehead and settled upon the bridge of his nose.

Holmes: It is a question of cubic capacity ... a man with so large a brain must have something in it.

Watson: The decline of his fortunes, then?

Holmes: This hat is three years old. These flat brims curled at the edge came in then. It is a hat of the very best quality. Look at the band of ribbed silk, and the excellent lining. If this man could afford to buy so expensive a hat three years ago, and has had no hat since, then he has assuredly gone down in the world.

Watson: Well, that is clear enough, certainly. But how about the foresight, and the moral retrogression?

Holmes: Here is the foresight . . . *[Holmes put] his finger upon the little disc and loop of the hat-securer.* They are never sold upon hats. If this man ordered one, it is a sign of a certain amount of foresight, since he went out of his way to take this precaution against the wind. But since we see that he has broken the elastic, and has not troubled to replace it, it is obvious that he has less foresight now than formerly, which is a distinct proof of a weakening nature. On the other hand, he has endeavoured to conceal some of these stains upon the felt by daubing them with ink, which is a sign that he has not entirely lost his self-respect. . . . The further points, that he is middle-aged, that his hair is grizzled, that it has been recently cut, and that he uses lime-cream, are all to be gathered from a close examination of the lower part of the lining. The [magnifying] lens discloses a large number of hair ends, clean cut by the scissors of the barber. They all appear to be adhesive, and there is a distinct odour of lime-cream. This dust, you will observe, is not the gritty, gray dust of the street but the fluffy brown dust of the house, showing that it has been hung up indoors most of the time, while the marks of moisture upon the inside are proof positive that the wearer perspired very freely, and could, therefore, hardly be in the best of training.

Watson: But his wife – you said that she had ceased to love him.

Holmes: This hat has not been brushed for weeks. When I see you, my dear Watson, with a week's accumulation of dust upon your hat, and when your wife allows you to go out in such a state, I shall fear that you also have been unfortunate enough to lose your wife's affection.

THE ART OF DISGUISE
Hats

A wardrobe of disguises is essential for any detective. Chief among these items are hats, for no single item of clothing changes one's appearance with as much ease and speed as a head covering. The added benefits of shading the eyes and concealing the hair cannot be underestimated.

The English do love their hats, and in Victorian London there were many types: bowlers (also called billycocks, cokes, and derbies), top hats, silk hats, opera hats, ascots, and boaters, to name a few. Depending on various factors – such as, most obviously, the time and place in which you live – you might include in your wardrobe of disguises: a babushka (scarflike headdress), for impersonating a Russian grandmother; a bellboy (pillbox cap), for a hotel employee (note that Billy the page also wore one of these); a fez (an upside-down felt flower pot with a tassel), if you find yourself in Morocco; a newsboy (short-brimmed beret), for a seller of newspapers; a ten-gallon (cowboy hat) for those in the American West; a topi (a wide-brimmed sun hat) for someone in India or the tropics; a weeper's hat (heavy black hatband) for attending funerals; and the deerstalker (a double-billed cap with earflaps), if you are attempting to impersonate the master detective Sherlock Holmes (though it's a little-known fact that he seldom wore one!). This list does not pretend to be comprehensive. Use your imagination to help you round out your disguise cabinet, and a good sourcebook on apparel can fill in any missing pieces.

Remember that different situations will require your hats to be in different stages of wear and tear (a well-maintained silk hat for a gentleman in the city, for example; the same hat more threadbare for a once respectable man now down on his luck). In order to obtain the desired effects, you might employ friends or family members to wear such a hat new until it shows appropriate signs of wear. And when you are ready to don the hat you have carefully chosen for your disguise, do make sure it fits properly. Nothing so much as ill fit will give away your cover.

Be thoughtful, be clever, and be convincing!

VICTORIAN CARRIAGES, COACHES, AND CARTS
How detectives and other citizens traveled

Ground transportation in early-nineteenth-century London was predominantly horse driven. By the late nineteenth century, railways covered England, which changed people's lives dramatically by allowing them to move greater distances in shorter periods of time. Railways affected city folk: suburbs formed around London, allowing people to work within the city, but live outside it. Within London, the first underground railway began service in 1863 as well.

Despite all of these advances, at the time of this story, city dwellers still used horse and carriage to move around London. Some of the carriages that existed have been described in this book. Like personal transportation of any age, the style in which people rode often reflected their status in society. The wealthy usually had their own carriages with a staff that maintained them and their horses. The lower classes owned carts at best or relied on public transport offered by hansoms, hackneys, and omnibuses. Vehicles of this time included the following:

Brougham:

An enclosed carriage sitting two to four passengers with a driver perched on the outside up front. Designed by Lord Brougham in the 1830s, it originally had two wheels, but had advanced to four by the time of this story. This carriage was pulled by one horse (though you might notice that Professor Moriarty had a modified two-horse Brougham, which was altered for greater speed).

Phaeton:

Named for the charioteer of classical myth, a light four-wheel carriage with open sides, bench seat, and drawn by one or two horses. This vehicle could move quite fast, had no designated seat for a driver, and was usually driven by the owner.

Victoria:

A variation of the Phaeton, also low and open with four

wheels. It sat one or two people, and was very popular with Victorian women because of its ease of access.

Coach:

Enclosed four-wheel vehicle, drawn by four to six horses. Coaches were generally quite large and were designed for long-distance travel.

Hansom Cab:

Named for Joseph Hansom who invented it in the 1830s, this two-wheeled vehicle-for-hire seated two people up front. There was an elevated seat in the rear for the driver, designed so that he would not obstruct the view of his passengers.

Hackney:

Also a vehicle-for-hire, the hackney was a retired coach that had once been owned by the well-to-do, and was usually drawn by a tired old horse. Its name derives from the word "hackneyed," meaning worn out to the point of becoming commonplace. Hackneys were licensed and regulated like modern-day taxis.

Omnibus:

A large horse-drawn vehicle that traveled fixed routes and could accommodate twenty-six people — twelve passengers inside, and fourteen on the roof.

Cart:

This vehicle had two wheels, was fitted with a single horse, and appeared with or without a top. Carts were generally quite heavy as they were designed for hauling loads of cargo. They sometimes carried people, but generally the lower classes.

ACKNOWLEDGMENTS

It is a mystery how this book could have materialized without the support and tireless efforts of many people. We would like to thank all of our friends and family who listened to us brainstorm and dream about the idea of this series for the past four years, and particularly Samantha Citrin, for the seemingly endless loan of her laptop, without which we surely would not have accomplished very much.

Untold thanks go to our agent Gail Hochman, insightful reader, sage counsel, and good friend; our editor, Lisa Sandell, for her intelligence, attentiveness, and calm; editorial director, Ken Geist, for his passion and immense creativity; Jean Feiwel, who believed in us and the Baker Street Irregulars from the first, and whose early vision continues to be a guiding light; our copyeditor, Anne Dunn, whose attention to detail would impress the Master himself; our fact-checker, Deirdre David, Professor Emerita of English, Temple University, for corroborating our research and keeping us on task; the brilliant Greg Ruth, for bringing our characters and their world so vividly and evocatively to life; Elizabeth Parisi, for her exquisite book design; David Saylor, for his thoughtful and inspired art direction; Jazan Higgins, for her boundless enthusiasm; Andrea Pinkney, for her great care and support; and Lisa Holton, a fellow Sherlockian, who has cheered us on from the very beginning.

And deepest thanks to our daughter, Ruby Citrin, for being such a good sleeper, and allowing us time to write.

— T. M. & M. C.

SHERLOCK HOLMES
and the BAKER STREET IRREGULARS

CASEBOOK № 2
Coming Summer 2007

Esteemed Reader,

If you have come this far, you are probably curious to know what the Baker Street Irregulars' next mystery will be. Rest assured their adventures are only just beginning!

In Casebook No. 2, a young woman, Elsa Hoff, seeks the services of Sherlock Holmes to investigate the strange circumstances surrounding the death of her aunt and benefactor, Greta Berlinger, and our boys are once again called to action.

Because you have proven yourself a loyal reader, I will share a few pertinent facts of the case: Elsa reports to Holmes that her aunt Greta—a wealthy woman with a passion for mysticism—had hired a teenage medium, Konstantin, to contact her long-deceased husband, Gunther. During the séance, Konstantin not only summoned the spirit of Gunther but actually produced him in bodily form. So shocked by her husband's physical appearance, Greta fell over dead.

You may recall from Casebook No. 1 that Sherlock Holmes believes only in science and reason and is skeptical about mysticism. Nevertheless, he agrees to look into the matter and calls on the Irregulars to conduct surveillance of Konstantin's lodgings—a decrepit old mansion in a quiet part of London.

The boys realize immediately that the mansion is haunted. As they keep watch, they notice that the inhabitants seem to materialize and then vaporize. And the adventure takes an even more dangerous turn when the boys discover that Elsa herself is being followed by shady-looking characters.

Is someone about to make an attempt on Elsa's life? Can Holmes and the Irregulars get to the bottom of the mystery without putting their own lives in jeopardy? Are Pilar's mystical powers able to aid them? And will Ozzie locate the father he has never known?

I must warn you: This story will take you into the eerie realm of the supernatural. Or is it into another dark underworld of crooks and conmen, thieves and murderers? Join us for this mysterious and frightening adventure and decide for yourself.

Yours anonymously

As Sherlock Holmes so artfully articulated, "Talent always recognizes genius." In that spirit, we would like to acknowledge the many fine minds working behind the scenes to create the first casebook of *Sherlock Holmes and the Baker Street Irregulars.* This volume was exquisitely designed by Elizabeth B. Parisi. The text type was set in 12-point Cloister Old Style, originally created in 1897 by Morris Fuller Benton. The display type was set in Penny Arcade, conceived in 1992 by Dan X. Solo. The book was printed and bound by the good people at R. R. Donnelly in Crawfordsville, Indiana. The manufacturing was deftly overseen by Angela Biola and Francine O'Bum.